And there it was, a fresh reminder of what Micah had most recently wreaked on her life, on her family.

She bent over and lifted the picture, careful not to disturb the broken glass, and realized that this day had gotten the best of her, that there just wasn't any more she could take.

"I'm not really hungry. I think I'll just go to bed."

"Aw, Lexie...please..."

"Good night," she answered unwaveringly before she took the picture and left him standing on the landing.

He was still there when she reached the guest room.

She could feel his eyes on her, but she didn't let that stop her as she went into the room and nudged the door closed behind her.

Things were the way they were.

And nothing could change them.

Or the way she felt about Micah because of it.

* * *

THE CAMDENS OF MONTANA: Four military brothers falling in love in Big Sky Country!

Dear Reader,

Yes, there *are* more Camdens out there! We're in the small town of Merritt, Montana, to meet the Denver Camdens' country cousins. First up is Micah.

Micah is fresh out of the marines and working hard to open a craft brewery. Everything is riding on it, when his childhood best friend, Lexie Parker, returns to Merritt.

Lexie is newly divorced and needs a fresh start. Micah is not in that plan. They parted ways when Micah's secret crush on her led him to do something that had consequences for Lexie that she's never forgiven. It doesn't matter to her that her grandmother thinks the world of Micah or that Gertie insists that the marines have made Micah a better man.

The trouble is, that *better man* is so very sorry for what he did years ago, and now he has sooo much more appeal than he did before.

But can she forgive him? Find out...

As always, happy reading!

Best,

Victoria Pade

The Marine Makes Amends

VICTORIA PADE

HARLEQUIN

SPECIAL
EDITION

**HARLEQUIN®
SPECIAL
EDITION™**

Recycling programs
for this product may
not exist in your area.

ISBN-13: 978-1-335-40461-9

The Marine Makes Amends

Copyright © 2020 by Victoria Pade

For questions and comments about the quality of this book, please contact us at CustomerService@Harlequin.com.

Harlequin Enterprises ULC
22 Adelaide St. West, 40th Floor
Toronto, Ontario M5H 4E3, Canada
www.Harlequin.com

Printed in U.S.A.

Victoria Pade is a *USA TODAY* bestselling author of numerous romance novels. She has two beautiful and talented daughters—Cori and Erin—and is a native of Colorado, where she lives and writes. A devoted chocolate lover, she's in search of the perfect chocolate-chip-cookie recipe.

For information about her latest and upcoming releases, visit Victoria Pade on Facebook—she would love to hear from you.

Chapter One

"Home again, home again…" Lexie Parker muttered to herself in relief as she headed for a restroom in the Billings, Montana, airport.

She wasn't quite home yet. Home was the small town of Merritt where she'd grown up. But this was the closest she'd been in over a decade.

"A little pit stop, get my luggage, rent a car and I'll be there, Gram," she said as if her grandmother could hear her.

It was the last Saturday in May and Lexie had been traveling since 3:00 a.m. If she'd waited for a direct flight, the trip from Anchorage, Alaska, would have taken approximately four and a half hours. Instead, she'd had to zigzag, enduring through two layovers, over the course of ten hours. But there was just no way she'd been willing to wait.

Her grandmother had had an accident yesterday that had badly broken the eighty-year-old's leg. Lexie had received a frantic call from their cousin Mary just as Gertie was being sent into surgery.

The surgery had gone well—so well that after spending the night in the hospital, Gertie had been released this morning. But still Lexie wanted to get to her grandmother. Ditching her original plan to move home from Anchorage ten days from now, Lexie had apologized to her boss for not finishing out her two-week notice, thrown everything she owned into two suitcases and rearranged her travel plans.

But the rush and the lengthy trip—not to mention the mess her life had been in for the last several months—showed on her face as she peered into the bathroom mirror.

"You look lousy," she told her reflection.

And not the way she wanted to look when she saw her very observant grandmother.

She decided it would be worth taking the time to spruce herself up before getting her bags and her rental car. Rushing to baggage claim wouldn't make her suitcases appear any faster.

Hair first, she decided, taking a hairbrush from

the floppy oversize purse she carried. She pulled her sloppy topknot free and flipped over to brush her hair from the bottom up.

It took a while to get the tangles out but she finally managed it, regathering the long thick strands into another topknot and tuck before replacing the hairpins.

Better, she judged when she glanced in the mirror again.

Being upside down had also helped put some color into her cheeks, though that was likely temporary. Since confronting Jason with her resolve to finally move back to Merritt—and the bombshell he'd dropped in response—Lexie had had friends and coworkers telling her she was pale. Normally, she didn't care, but it was something else she didn't want her grandmother to see.

So she fished around in her purse for some emergency makeup, digging out blotting papers, a well-used blush compact, a tube of mascara and an almost-used-up eyeliner pencil.

One of the blotting sheets went to work first, followed by just a hint of the blush on the apples of high cheekbones that were a bit more pronounced since stress had stolen her appetite.

Next she used the eyeliner, making a single thin line on the top of both lids, following that up with mascara to help bring out her silver-gray eyes and make her look less weary.

As she smoothed her ring fingertips over her dark eyebrows, her eyes were drawn to the lack of her wedding ring.

She'd taken the band off not long after filing for divorce five months ago and had stopped feeling naked without it—and yet right now, she felt so aware of the absence of it again. But she reminded herself that this was the beginning of her fresh start and that that was a good thing.

A fresh start, she repeated silently to remind herself of her goal.

Exhaling slowly, she shoved away thoughts of her past as she took a tinted lip gloss from her purse and applied it to lips that were just full enough and just rosy enough not to need more than gloss.

Better, was her decree when she moved her head from side to side to judge her handiwork.

From there she switched her focus to her clothes.

Her jeans were fine but the yellow turtleneck was making her too warm. Late May in Merritt meant warmer temperatures than she'd find in Anchorage, and she hadn't planned ahead.

But she didn't have a change of shirts in her purse so the best she could do now was smooth out the shirt's wrinkles and push the sleeves above her elbows.

"That's as good as it's going to get," she told

her reflection, slinging the strap of her purse over her shoulder to leave the restroom.

She wasn't far from baggage claim and went directly there, seeing that even with her restroom delay, no luggage had come onto the carousel yet.

She took a spot among the other passengers.

Any minute, folks, I want to get where I'm going...

"Lexie?"

The sound of her name startled her and she shot a glance to her left.

She locked eyes with the owner of the deep male voice, who then said, "Yep, that's you. I thought so. Gertie was right—you haven't changed..."

It took Lexie a moment to register that she recognized the man. And then came the sinking feeling when she noticed that he didn't have the air of a traveler about him—no luggage or carry-ons or reading materials.

Instead, he gave the impression that he might be there to pick someone up. The fact that his attention was on her and that he'd mentioned her grandmother's name made her instantly afraid that that someone might be her.

The man was Micah Camden and since the first week of their senior year in high school, she'd regretted ever having known him.

Old anger and resentment zoomed through her but she worked to keep it out of her voice when she said, "Odd to see you here..."

"I've been with Gertie and Mary since yester-day," he responded. "Mary said you were going to rent a car to drive to Merritt and Gertie didn't like that idea, so I came down to get you."

"She must be on a lot of drugs." *To send you, of all people*, Lexie thought.

The sound of the baggage carousel starting up drew his attention away from her. But Lexie con-tinued to glare at him, frozen in disbelief that her grandmother would send Micah Camden.

A moment later, he turned his still-striking co-balt blue eyes back to her and said, "You don't have to take me up on the ride, if you don't want to. You can still rent a car and I can just follow you to town so Gertie knows I'm at least watching out for you."

That was an idea. Then she wouldn't have to be in an enclosed space with him for the hour it would take to get to Merritt. She wouldn't have to talk to him.

It was tempting.

But frugality was one of the things she'd learned well over the years and renting a car was not cheap. It even seemed a little frivolous, since once she got to town, she could drive her grandmother's car or truck until she could afford something of her own—but it had been the quickest way to get there.

Until now, when Micah Camden was giving her another option.

An option that irked her even though it was to her benefit.

She tried not to show too much of her irritation. "Renting a car if I don't have to would be a waste of money," she admitted reluctantly.

He nodded but didn't say anything else as she caught sight of the smaller of her suitcases.

Without saying anything else to him, she stepped over to scoop the duffel-like bag off and stayed where she was just to get some distance from Micah Camden as this situation sank in.

Until fifteen years ago, she'd considered him one of her three best friends. *The Four Musketeers*—that's what everyone had called them growing up. Lexie, Jason Lundy, Jill Gunner and *him*.

But fifteen years ago, Micah Camden had proven he was no friend at all. Not to her. Not to Jason. For the remaining two years Lexie had been in Merritt, she'd had nothing to do with him, and since leaving she'd put any thought of him out of her mind altogether.

And now here he was.

He'd said she looked the same and so did he. Only better, if that were possible, she thought begrudgingly as she secretly studied him.

The Camden brothers—all four of them—were known for a few things. Their good looks topped the list.

When it came to Micah, that meant coarse

brown-almost-black hair that he now wore crisply short over his very square forehead.

His undeniably handsome face was angular, with a straight, perfect nose poised between high cheekbones and a razor-sharp jawline that currently had a hint of five o'clock shadow that Lexie refused to admit was rugged and sexy.

His intensely masculine face was softened only by those blue eyes.

Those eyes…

Beneath a shelf of faintly unruly eyebrows, they were a little deep-set—just enough to somehow emphasize the color that was so remarkable and so distinctive to his family that there were actually articles written about *The Camden Blue Eyes*, focusing on his cousins, the higher-profiled Camdens in Denver who owned Camden Superstores.

Those eyes that were so blue, so bright, it was difficult not to stare at them. They hardly seemed real.

But real they were and Lexie forced herself to stop staring at them, moving on instead to his mouth in hopes of finding some fault there.

Nope, she couldn't find a flaw there, either. His lips were male-model impeccable, giving no evidence of the lies that could spew from them.

No, time hadn't diminished how drop-dead gorgeous he was. If anything, the added maturity had honed and added to his appeal.

And the body that went with the face and hair?

The last time she'd seen him it had been barely more than a boy's body. But over the years, he'd gained some height—at least three inches over the six feet he'd been. And now, barely contained by a military blue crewneck T-shirt, he had shoulders a mile wide, pecs that filled the knit impressively and wowza-biceps that stretched the short sleeves to their limits.

Below that were jeans that traced narrow hips and clung to sturdy tree-trunk thighs that made it seem as if nothing could make him fall.

Unlike the actual tree he'd crashed into her grandmother's house…

Lexie averted her eyes and concentrated on the bags coming out along the carousel.

Her main bag was approaching, and because she'd needed it to carry the lion's share of what she owned from one move to the other, it was trunk-sized. When she tried to grab it, Micah reached in front of her, saying, "Let me do that."

It was on the tip of her tongue to say *no* but too many times her recovery of that suitcase had been less than graceful, so she just let him. But as soon as he had it off the carousel she took over, pulling up the bar handle and tipping it onto its wheels.

"Sooo, the verdict is that you're going to let me take you to Merritt?" Micah asked.

His voice was lower than she remembered it.

And there was something strong and confident in his tone, too, as if her agreement was a foregone conclusion.

And, damn him, it was.

"I guess so," she answered with resignation.

He nodded agreeably—not victoriously—which was a good thing because Lexie might have accepted the ride but she wasn't conceding anything.

Fifteen years ago, he'd shown her his true colors.

And that was when she'd learned that he was an A-one jerk who couldn't be trusted.

After they loaded up Micah's big white pickup truck and finally got on the highway, Lexie tried to put her dislike of Micah Camden aside enough to get some answers about her grandmother and what had happened to cause Gertrude Parker's injury.

"*Is* Gram doing well enough not to be in the hospital or did she just refuse to stay?" she asked.

"She's doing great. By this morning when she asked if she could go home, the doctors didn't see any reason not to release her. She might have a lot of years under her belt, but you know how she is—she's a firecracker, she has spunk."

"I just don't want that to override anyone's better judgment about her health. She's *eighty* years old."

"I don't think she was fooling anybody. The surgeon and the orthopedist came over from Northbridge."

Lexie let out a sigh of relief. Northbridge was a fairly small town, but it had a bigger hospital than Merritt, making it able to sustain a few specialists. If Gram's doctor had called them in, then that meant they were taking the situation seriously.

"By this morning, they signed off on her leaving the hospital. Plus, her local doctor came in to talk to them and agreed. So Mary and I checked her out. And you know Merritt, it isn't like a big city—house calls aren't unusual. Joan—Gertie's regular doc—said she'd stop in every day for a while to check on her."

Lexie's worries weren't completely allayed—they wouldn't be until she saw for herself that her grandmother was all right—but she relaxed enough to ask the other question on her mind.

"What exactly happened?"

"You know I'm renting Gertie's barn as my brewery?"

Lexie knew, all right—and she considered it a deal with the devil.

"Yes, she told me she decided to rent you the barn the way she leases the fields to the neighbors now that she can't work the farm anymore."

"Right. Well, I'm using the space for a small craft brewery. Gertie is actually my adviser and my taste tester—not that that has anything to do with this. There wasn't any tasting going on when she got hurt," he added in a hurry.

Lexie knew Gertie well enough to know she only ever drank in moderation. And besides, after a lifetime of hobby brewing, she could handle what she did drink.

"Anyway," Micah continued, "I was having a new forklift delivered and it got away from the guy who was unloading it. It hit that tree that stands between Gertie's place and the little house—"

"*My* house—the house my dad built next door for him and Mom and me? The house where I'm going to live? It was involved in this, too?" Lexie demanded, alarmed.

"Yeah…well…" Micah said, clearly uncomfortable, "the forklift hit the tree and it went down. It took out the side wall of Gertie's house, and uh…a pretty good chunk of the little house…"

"*A pretty good chunk* of the little house? More than just a side wall?"

"There's damage all the way around," he answered reluctantly. Then, as if to avoid getting into more of that, he returned to her original question about her grandmother's injury.

"Luckily, Gertie was downstairs when the tree went down, on the opposite end of the living room—which was untouched, by the way. But she didn't know what had happened and she ran like a bat out of hell out the front door. She was in such a hurry that she tripped going down the porch steps and fell."

"Don't make it sound like it was her fault!"

"I didn't mean to," he assured her. "Of course, it wasn't her fault. She was scared—rightfully so— and ran out just like anybody would have. When she fell, her leg twisted out from under her, and the lower part of her femur caught the brunt of it."

He *was* just stating facts but Lexie was already upset about her grandmother. Learning that the house she'd expected to come home to was also a casualty pushed her unhappiness that much further.

Then, as she thought about her house and her grandmother's, something else occurred to her.

"How could Gram go home to a house without a side wall?"

"Actually it's the stairs that made returning to her house impossible," he informed. "The surgery put a plate and four screws in her femur—"

"Mary told me that."

"Well, the leg is in a cast and it has to be raised and stationary for a while. So they want her in a wheelchair for now. She can't be anywhere where she'd have to navigate stairs—"

"Or, I would assume, any house that's missing a wall."

"Well, yeah…"

"So where did Gram go home to?" Lexie demanded.

"Mary's apartment. It's tiny but there are two bedrooms and she really wanted Gertie to stay with her. She said she's bored and lonely and she'd be happy for the company. And she's a retired nurse, you know, so she's a good choice for taking care of Gertie. Plus, with the apartment in the heart of town, Gertie is closer to the hospital if anything goes wrong, and the apartment is easy for Joan to get to for house calls. So Gertie and Mary decided they're going to be roomies until Gertie's place is fixed and Gertie can handle that layout."

Mary had been in her apartment for as long as Lexie could remember so Lexie knew it wasn't big enough to house her, too, and she suddenly wondered if she was homeless.

Yet another unpleasant revelation from this guy…

She took a breath and focused on what was most important. "Okay, that sounds like a decent arrangement for them."

"I think it is," he said, sounding relieved that she wasn't kicking up more of a fuss.

"But," Lexie said then, "I was going to move into the little house—*my* house. Did the *pretty good chunk* taken out of it make that impossible?"

"It did," he confirmed, sounding guilty. "But," he added in a hurry and in a more positive tone, "I had both places inspected this morning by county inspectors. And while the little house can't be lived in yet, most of the damage to Gertie's house is really concentrated in that one spot. The rest of the big house is structurally sound, and has been cleared for occupancy. So you can move in there."

"With a gaping hole that could let anyone just walk in any time of the day or night," she said more to herself than to him.

"That's taken care of, too," he assured her.

"*How* is that taken care of, too?"

"I had the open side of the house tarped and I promised Gertie that I'll move into the sunroom downstairs and stay there so I can make sure there's no looting—and no kids trying to use it as a party spot..."

Was he honestly telling her what it seemed like he was telling her?

"*You* and *I* are going to be *housemates*?" she said, her voice louder than she'd intended it to be.

"You'll be upstairs, I'll be down—in the sunroom that's not really *in* the house. I'll use the bathroom downstairs. You'll have the one upstairs to yourself. I'll never even climb the stairs..."

"And we know how you like to take that kind of situation and spin it for your own benefit," she said, this time keeping none of her animosity toward him hidden.

That left a heavy silence for a moment before a

much more subdued Micah said in a somber voice, "I can never tell you how sorry—"

"As if that matters!" Lexie snapped, cutting him off. She was in no mood to hear apologies or re-hash the past with him.

Instead, as they approached the sign welcoming them to Merritt, she turned her head to glare at him again and added, "Don't forget that I *know* you. And don't think for one minute that I won't be watching your every move."

He nodded his head, accepting that with every indication of resignation.

Lexie went on glowering at him, furious with the situation but not seeing any way out. The one person on earth she didn't even want to know existed was the person she was going to be cohabitating with. And worst of all, this was putting her in a position similar to the one he'd used to cause trouble for her fifteen years ago.

This was *not* what she'd wanted to come home to.

But, unlike the rental car, in this she didn't have any choice.

She couldn't afford a room at the bed-and-breakfast that was the only temporary option in town and she certainly couldn't pay for an apart-ment of her own. And while she could insist on him leaving her to stay by herself, she didn't like the idea of being alone in a house that anyone could walk into day or night. She had a feeling Gram wouldn't like the idea of that, either, and Lexie didn't feel as if she could add any more stress to her ailing grandmother by pitching a fit about it.

So she was going to have to put her own negative feelings about him on the back burner and make the best of a rotten situation.

But there would be no forgetting that even if Micah Camden had grown up to be as head-turningly handsome a man as she had ever seen, underneath that very impressive surface was nothing good.

Chapter Two

The drive from the airport in Billings to Merritt took until nearly four thirty Saturday afternoon. When Micah pulled up in front of the fourplex where Gertie was staying with her cousin, he asked Lexie if she wanted time alone with her grandmother and offered to wait in his truck if she did.

Lexie took him up on the offer so that left him with plenty of time to kill, sitting in the cab of his pickup truck and thinking that he must be getting soft. On active duty in the Marines, there had been more than one training mission that had cost him plenty of sleep. None of those had left him feeling as tired as he was now, even though all he'd done last night was sit in a chair in Gertie's hospital room.

Fighting his exhaustion didn't serve any purpose, though, so he closed his eyes and laid his head back against the seat.

He'd been told there was no need for him to stay last night but he'd still refused to leave. Gertie was eighty years old with a broken leg and had just undergone emergency surgery. She'd been groggy from the anesthesia and he'd been afraid she wouldn't have the wherewithal to ring for a nurse if she woke and needed care.

While he and Gertie might not literally be family, Gertie was still like family to him. Anything he would do for his brothers or his own grandfather, he would do for her. There was no question about it.

Add to that the fact that it was *his* runaway forklift that had caused this whole mess and there was all the more reason for him to make sure that whatever Gertie needed, Gertie got.

He hated that she'd been hurt at all, let alone over anything to do with him or his business.

"Damn it all to hell," he cursed for the hundredth time since it had happened, struggling under the weight of his guilt, wishing he were the one with the broken bone instead of Gertie.

Gertie, who had only ever been kind, generous, caring, compassionate and even sympathetic to him when he hadn't deserved it. When she'd had every reason to just write him off.

But somehow Gertie had found it in herself to forgive him.

Unlike Lexie, he thought ruefully.

The past hour had proven that her feelings for him, her opinion of him, definitely weren't any better now than all those years ago.

He understood that. He'd done something truly lousy that had caused a domino effect of problems. It hadn't been his intention to hurt anyone. But what he *had* intended had been purely self-serving and it had avalanched. Directly onto her.

He wasn't the same person he'd been then, the person his mother had raised him—and his three brothers—to be. The Marines had taken that raw material full of not altogether good values that his mother had given him and used it to make him into what he hoped was a better man.

But all Lexie knew was the person he'd been before the Marines taught him honor and integrity, loyalty, brotherhood and unity. All Lexie knew was the boy who'd had only a vague acquaintance with those things and so had brought disaster into her young life.

Disaster that had hurt her in particular, and cost him his friendship with her and with Jason. Friendships that had begun in preschool.

Hell, his singlemindedness was still costing

him, he thought. Most recently, he'd paid the price for it with Adrianna—even when he'd been sure he was doing everything right with his former significant other...

Tired or not, his racing mind wasn't letting him rest, so he lifted his head from the back of the seat and opened his eyes.

There was nothing he could do to rectify the current fallout with Adrianna. But he *was* going to make sure every inch of Gertie's and Lexie's property was fixed as good as new. And maybe in the meantime he could find a way to atone for the ugly part of his history with Lexie, too.

You didn't let me say it, but you can never know how sorry I am...

He'd just been so young and immature. And brainwashed.

And so damn head over heels, wildly and hopelessly crushing on Lexie for four years by that point—ever since the end of seventh grade—up until that day when it had stupidly seemed to him like an opportunity had finally presented itself.

Until the end of seventh grade, Jason, the boy next door; Lexie, the part tomboy, part sweetheart; Jill, the bookish, analytical mouse; and Micah, the push-the-limits smart-ass, had been inseparable best friends. They'd done everything together, and Micah hadn't felt anything but friendship for any one of them. It had been clear-cut.

And then little by little it had started to be confusing...

By the summer before eighth grade—about when his voice had cracked and he'd sprouted up five inches overnight—he'd begun to notice that he wanted to be with Lexie more than he wanted to be with Jill or even Jason. That he wanted to be alone with Lexie.

Little by little, he'd started to take note of things about Lexie that he didn't notice about Jason or Jill.

Lexie's hair. Lexie's eyes. Lexie's laugh—and how good it made him feel if he could *make* her laugh...

He hadn't understood what was going on at first—not until his brother Quinn figured it out and teased him about wanting Lexie to be his *girlfriend*.

He'd denied it, of course. Punched Quinn for laughing at him. And told himself that Quinn was wrong. But eventually he'd begun to realize that Quinn wasn't wrong.

The trouble was, about the time Micah had accepted that he might like Lexie as more than a friend, Jason had gotten on the same track.

At first it was as subtle as two thirteen-year-old boys could be—posturing, vying awkwardly for her attention, competing with each other, horsing around in order to entertain her.

They'd jockeyed for which of them could persuade her to study with him or do a school project with him. They'd both tried to be the first at her door in the morning to walk her to the bus stop. They'd wrestled to be the one to snag a seat next to her on the bus.

But over time, Jason had developed some game—he'd learned to flirt and his adolescent edges had smoothed out.

While Micah's hadn't.

Suddenly—or at least it had seemed sudden to Micah—Jason and Lexie started to have private jokes that neither Micah nor Jill had been privy to. Suddenly Jason was bold enough to whisper in Lexie's ear, sharing secrets just for them. Suddenly Jason was making her smile and giggle in a way Micah wasn't.

Before Micah knew it, there was something between Jason and Lexie that he couldn't quite seem to have with her.

And every time he watched Lexie with Jason, it tore his heart out.

You guys thought you were soul mates. What happened to that? Micah wondered, recalling how their young romance had developed while he'd watched from the sidelines, tortured by it…

It had taken years even after they'd all gone their separate ways for him to move on to the point where he could hope they were happy together.

But apparently that wasn't how things had played out. He knew now, through Gertie, that Lexie and Jason had just divorced. He was sorry for both of his former friends. Genuinely sorry.

And the fact that his first glimpse of Lexie at the airport this afternoon had given him a split-second flashback to his childhood crush?

That was only a memory, too. It didn't mean anything. He'd moved so far beyond those old days, those old longings for her, that a fleeting moment of recollection was all it *could* be.

The door to Mary's apartment opened just then and out came Mary and Lexie.

As they paused there to talk on the front porch, Micah watched them.

Well, not *them*—it wasn't white-haired Mary he was focused on. It was only Lexie.

In the two years between when he'd wrecked their friendship and when Lexie and Jason had left Merritt, Lexie had avoided him as much as possible. But he'd gone on stealing any glimpse of her he could get, so he knew that her looks hadn't altered any during that time.

But add another thirteen years?

He'd recognized her at baggage claim the minute he laid eyes on her, so when he'd told her she hadn't changed, he'd meant it.

But there *were* changes, he realized.

Changes that were all improvements.

And he couldn't help taking in every detail one by one.

Her hair was the same rich russet brown, shining reddish wherever the spring sunlight hit it. She'd cut it to chin length at the end of high school but now, judging by the scale of that knot wrangled at the crown of her head, he could tell that if she let it loose it would again be long and thick and luxurious. The way he'd liked it.

The years had refined and perfected her face. The pretty girl had become all-out beautiful.

Her skin was pure peaches and cream—flawless, without a hint of teenage blemishes, and so smooth and velvety that it couldn't possibly feel as soft as it looked.

She'd always had a refined bone structure—a straight delicate nose, high cheekbones, a patrician jaw that hammocked a perky chin. But now it was all more elegant-looking.

Her ears were still just right—small, close to her head and cute—with lobes he'd pictured himself tugging on with his teeth. And the neck that she'd always complained was gawky now just looked long and graceful. The neck that, in his obsessed youth, he'd fantasized about kissing.

Though not as much as he'd fantasized kissing those lips…

Plush petal pink lips that could expand into a smile warm enough to melt glaciers.

He didn't know if that had changed because nothing about their reunion today had brought it out.

And then there were her superhero-colored eyes, he thought with a laugh, recalling the moment she'd turned them to him at the airport.

He'd coined the phrase *superhero color* to describe them back when he'd first become infatuated with her—gray eyes that were streaked with so much luminous silver that they seemed something more than mortal.

The silver streaks only seemed to have brightened to make her eyes all the more sparkling, all the more mesmerizing…

Okay, yes, for maybe the span of one breath he'd felt mesmerized at his first sight of them again. But they were stunning eyes. Anybody would have been momentarily struck by an initial glimpse.

It had been only for an instant, though. Then he'd come out of it…and noticed the rest of her.

She was dressed in a turtleneck and jeans that were both just snug enough to accentuate a body that was even better than when he'd seen her last.

Curves that had filled out in a way that made it hard not to stare.

Oh, yeah, she'd definitely gotten better, he decided. Much better, really.

And you let her go? he mentally asked his childhood friend in disbelief.

It seemed hard to fathom—though not because he had any designs on her, he was quick to remind himself. No designs. No feelings. No nothing. Because when it came to Lexie, they were just...

Well, he didn't know what they were.

She hadn't seen him as anything except a friend when he was lovesick over her, and he'd long since lost her friendship. Whatever they were now, it wasn't anything good.

On the other hand, his relationship with her grandmother was important to him. So important to him that he didn't want to lose either the personal or the professional part of it under any circumstances.

So not only was it vital that he make peace with Lexie over what he'd done fifteen years ago just to right the wrong, he thought that it was also essential that he try to reach some sort of civility with her in order not to damage his friendship and association with Gertie.

If he didn't, Lexie's opinion of him might muddy the waters with Gertie.

"Honest to God, Lexie, I'm not the person I was then," he said quietly.

But he knew mere words weren't enough now.

He was going to have to prove it to her.

He wasn't sure exactly how he was going to do that, but no matter what it took, he'd find a way.

Because even beyond his relationship with

Gertie, It would be nice if they could live in the small town together again without Lexie completely hating his guts.

Lexie had very little to say to Micah when she returned to his truck. In answer to his immediate question about how Gertie was doing, she told him that Gertie *said* she was doing well and that Mary had confirmed it.

But to Lexie, seeing her grandmother lying in bed, sleepy from the pain pill she'd taken just before Lexie's arrival, had been a painful blow. Gertie had looked so pale, so frail and so much older than she seemed when she was up and about, and being her usual feisty self. Lexie was left shaken and certainly not reassured that everything was as good as the two elderly women said it was.

Still, both her grandmother and their cousin had maintained that what Gertie needed most tonight was rest, and had insisted that Lexie go home, settle in and come back in the morning. Gertie had been especially intent on Lexie getting to the house to check out the damage so she could report back to her.

So after more of Mary's promises that everything really was fine and that she'd call should Gertie need Lexie in any way, Lexie was once again in Micah's passenger seat, not feeling any less worried than she had been before, and those worries continued to occupy her thoughts as they drove.

After a brief stop at the general store, where Micah ran in while Lexie stayed put so her luggage in the open truck bed in back wouldn't be left unattended, he took her home.

The property that had been in her family for generations, where she'd grown up, was just outside Merritt. She was braced for the damage that Micah had described, but it was still strange and awkward to arrive and see it looking like anything but the peaceful place she was familiar with.

Instead, the driveway was crowded with two other pickup trucks and a large wood-hauling truck, and a crew of six men were working on the downed tree between the houses.

The sounds of chain saws cutting through the tree, axes chopping what had already been cut and loud thunks as wood was thrown into the bed of the wood-hauling truck greeted them as they headed up the drive. And the huge oak tree that had towered above the houses—both the large two-story white farmhouse and the smaller version of it next door—was missing from the skyline Lexie had always known.

She hadn't really considered the mechanical details that cleanup and repair might entail. But seeing the size of the tree just made her dread all the more the moment when she'd finally see the damage to the houses.

"They're already demolishing the tree?" she said with some surprise, not having any idea what first step needed to be taken—or a second or third, for that matter—but somehow feeling as if it were too soon for so much to be going on.

"Yeah. I called this company in from Northbridge. They've been here since early this morning," Micah answered. "They got the limbs out of the houses first so I could put up tarps before I left for the airport—"

"There were tree limbs *inside* the houses…" she said, for some reason not having considered that before.

"Oh, yeah," Micah responded. "Once those were cut off and hauled out, they started to deal with the bigger part—most of the tree landed between the two houses. But from the looks of what they have loaded in that big truck, I'd say they're about done. Well, with this part. I'm having them move all the wood out behind the barn for now. When the repairs to the houses are finished and we're headed into winter, I'll bring it back to the woodpile so Gertie—and you—can use it for firewood."

Lexie nodded. She hadn't really thought that far ahead so it was good that someone was.

She was at the end of a very long day and hours

and hours of traveling. She'd just seen her ailing and weakened grandmother and nothing about that had eased her worries. And now this. It was a lot to contend with and she felt a little dazed by the magnitude of it all.

"How about we get you and your bags inside, and when you're ready, we can eat the dinner I got for us at the store?" Micah suggested then, speaking gently, as if he realized she'd reached her limit.

Lexie could only lift her chin slightly to agree.

She dragged her gaze from the work that was being done, gathered her purse and got out of the pickup at the same time as Micah. He took both of her suitcases from the truck bed and even Lexie's foggy brain couldn't help noticing how easily he wielded the weight of her heavy luggage and the way his enormous biceps stretched the short sleeves of his T-shirt as he hoisted the trunk over the sides of the truck.

When she realized what was going through her mind, she forced herself to look elsewhere and tamped down on the unwelcome appreciation of that view. Instead, she looked down at the ground as they approached the big house where he ushered her up the four porch steps and through the front door.

Once inside, the damage to the house became more evident even as Micah said, "I picked up all the tree rubble and swept, so it wouldn't be *too* dirty, but there's still some mess I didn't have a chance to get to..."

Straight ahead was the wide staircase with its stained wood steps that rose to the second floor. And although the stairs were clean, the family photos hung on the side wall were all askew.

In the big living room to the right were two overturned tables, lying on the floor next to fallen books and knickknacks. The two overstuffed easy chairs seemed to have jumped out of their usual positions, marked by indentations left in the tan carpeting inches away.

To the left of the entrance, though, was the kitchen. And that told an even harsher story.

Hazy light poured in through the tarp that covered a jagged edge around a great big hole where a wall used to be. The cupboards that had lined that wall were crushed and splintered where they'd fallen to the kitchen floor, their contents scattered and broken there, too.

"I know it looks bad," Micah said when he saw her stare in that direction. "But at least the appliances and the pipes and sink weren't affected. I had to turn off the electrical breaker to that outer wall but that's it," he downplayed.

Then, as if he didn't want her looking too closely at it, he hustled her upstairs where too much light was also coming from the door to her grandmother's bedroom, also to the left of the landing.

Lexie went as far as the doorway to peer inside and found the bedroom's hardwood floor had turned into a fragmented cliff up against the tarp there, while the bureau and the outer wall of the closet were missing. Clothes from both the closet and the bureau were piled near the side of the double bed, dusted with debris.

"Definitely a mess," she murmured.

Micah didn't say anything to that.

But just then there was a knock on the front door downstairs, immediately followed by the sound of it being opened as a male voice called, "Uh, do you want to show us where exactly to put the wood?"

"Be right there," Micah called back, looking to Lexie. "Unless you need me..."

"Does the shower in the guest room work?" she asked.

"It does. None of the plumbing was damaged," he reiterated.

"Then I'd like a shower. So do whatever you need to do—"

"And we'll meet downstairs when you're ready to eat," he concluded.

"Sure," she said unenthusiastically.

Micah bent over to pick up the luggage he'd set on the landing. Seeing that, she added, "You can leave those. I'll take them to the bedroom."

Micah nodded and stepped back, retracing his steps down the stairs.

Once he was gone, Lexie gave in to the urge to bend over and retrieve a framed photograph of her late grandfather from where it had crashed onto the floor.

It was a black-and-white picture of him smiling proudly as he stood beside a new tractor. The glass over the picture was cracked but still held in place by the frame. Lexie hooked the photograph back on the nail it had hung from for decades, making sure it was squarely in place.

Then she picked up the smaller of her bags, tipped the larger onto its wheels and headed for the guest room.

And with as many things as she *could* have been thinking about at that moment, somehow what came to mind suddenly was the image of Micah's bulging biceps.

She shoved the thought away and reminded herself that for the second time in her life, he was to blame for complications and hardships that she would have to deal with.

"I know this is a sore subject. But I'd like to talk about…fifteen years ago…"

Oh, this guy is pushing his luck with me today, Lexie thought.

A shower, a clean pair of yoga pants and a light-weight T-shirt had helped revitalize her somewhat.

While her hair had air-dried—and because her grandmother had told her to—she'd put clean sheets on the guest bed and then unpacked a few things.

When she'd come across her makeup bag, she'd been a little tempted to reapply at least some eye-liner and blush. But she'd resisted the urge. Why should she care what she looked like for *him*? And since she didn't, she'd left her face bare.

She had brushed out her hair, though. And for some reason, her rebellious side hadn't been strong enough to convince her to tie it back. Instead, she'd left it the way it looked best—falling the full six inches below her shoulders into the natural waves that air-drying gave it.

About that time, she'd heard the sounds of the workmen's trucks driving away from the farm, so she'd left the bedroom to come to the kitchen.

Micah had been standing at the unscathed round oak kitchen table unpacking the brown paper sack from the general store.

As he'd set out napkins and plastic forks, he explained that the general store now sold gourmet sandwiches along with their own macaroni and potato salads, and that that was what he'd bought for their dinner.

The sandwiches were grilled ciabatta bread

stacked high with pot roast, bacon, avocado, lettuce, tomato, cheddar and Monterey Jack cheese. Lexie had offered to pay for her share but he refused. She'd thanked him stiltedly and had just taken a bite when Micah had cut right to the chase with his sore-subject intro.

"I don't know what there is to talk about," Lexie responded flatly. "What you did, you did. It can't be undone so what's the point of going over it?"

Their senior year of high school had found them in the same science class. The first week, they'd partnered on a project that had sent them to an abandoned farm to collect vegetation samples.

Caught in a severe hailstorm, they'd had to run for the barn, crawling under a barbed wire fence in their hurry to get there. The loose blouse Lexie had had on had caught on the barbs and gotten ripped into wet shreds.

Micah had been dressed in a jean jacket over one of the many barely appropriate death metal band T-shirts he was known to wear, and since the T-shirt was moderately dry, thanks to the jacket's protection, he'd taken it off and given it to Lexie to change into in the barn's tack room.

The only thing that had transpired during their hour wait for the storm to end was a game to see which of them could throw the most rocks into an old tin can.

Then the rain and hail had stopped and they'd

emerged from the barn—Lexie dressed in Micah's T-shirt, and Micah with his chest exposed under his jean jacket.

At just that moment, one of the school buses had passed by carrying the gymnastics team. Windows had been lowered and heads had popped out to call out lewd questions about what the two of them had been up to.

By the next day, the story of them emerging from the barn had circulated and grown, with everyone believing that a whole lot more had gone on between them than merely waiting out a hailstorm.

And Micah hadn't denied it.

In fact, after a few times of merely smiling when he was asked about it, he'd begun to encourage the rumors, nodding as if to confirm the suspicions that he'd hooked up with Lexie in the barn.

Even if it had been just that, it would have been bad enough.

But gossip about them traveled through town like wildfire and while Jason had believed Lexie when she'd told him nothing happened— despite Micah only replying, *Wouldn't you like to know?* when Jason had confronted him—Lexie's extremely overprotective father had doubted her.

He'd torn her room apart, searched her computer, read her diary. And while he hadn't discovered evidence of more than a friendship with

Micah, he *had* discovered enough to reveal that she and Jason were having sex.

Lexie's father had hit the ceiling. He'd pulled her out of the local school and shipped her off to an all-girls religious academy for the rest of her senior year, putting her under house arrest when she was home on weekends.

"I need to tell you how sorry I am," Micah said.

"Too little, too late."

"I know. And I don't have any excuses—"

"Good, because there aren't any that can make what you did okay. You wrecked my senior year. I got stuck in a *boarding* school during the week, with girls who only saw me as an outsider. I didn't get to go to football games or homecoming or prom or anything else I was looking forward to. I didn't get to graduate with my friends, with the kids I'd been with since kindergarten. And when I was home, I was under constant watch by both my parents. My relationship with my father turned so…" She sighed angrily. "We fought so much. He was so disappointed in me. So…"

Lexie glared at Micah. "You know how he was—he was an altar boy as a kid. He considered being a priest. To him, it was a huge deal that I stay *pure* until marriage. Jason and I were sure we were getting married, so to us it was okay that we didn't wait for a wedding night… And we'd been so careful—my dad would never have known. But when he found out—" Lexie's voice cracked when she thought about her dad, her own regrets resurging that she hadn't maintained her virginity when it had been so important to him "—it changed *everything* between us. And it never went back to how it had been."

She fought tears over what had been so much more of a loss to her than football games or dances, focusing on her anger instead. "Jason and I *eloped* because my dad wouldn't walk me down the aisle of a church!" she shouted at Micah. "He *died* thinking of me as…not what he wanted his daughter to be. And all of it—*all* of it— was because of a misunderstanding that *you* wouldn't deny. That you *encouraged*! And why was that, Micah?" she demanded. "Because it made you feel like a big man? A stud?"

Micah closed his eyes and absorbed her rancor stoically. Then he opened them and shook his head. "There were so many reasons—but not one of them was reason enough to do that to you. To cost you all of that. And it's been the biggest regret of my life. The thing I'm most ashamed of," he admitted so quietly it was barely audible.

Lexie stared at him. His words, the tone of his voice, the expression on his handsome face, the look in his eyes didn't allow her to doubt that he genuinely meant what he said. And she knew that if she were an impartial third party in this moment, her heart would go out to him. That she would think, *How could anyone not forgive someone who's showing so much remorse?*

But she wasn't an impartial third party.

Until he'd done what he'd done, caused what he'd caused, she'd been the apple of her father's eye. A daddy's girl through and through.

Afterward, she couldn't remember her father even looking her *in* the eye again.

And then he and her mother had died in a car accident before their relationship had had a chance to heal, to evolve beyond it. With time, maybe her dad would have come to grips with the idea of her as a grown woman, an adult, a sexual being.

Instead, his life had ended and so had any chance for them to reconcile.

So Lexie wasn't an impartial third party. And the shame that *she'd* felt with her father was something she still carried with her. Something she was convinced she always *would* carry with her.

No matter how deep and sincere his regret, Micah had put into motion things that could never be set right again.

She didn't know what he expected her to say at that moment. It couldn't be that she forgave him, if that was what he was looking for. But she also discovered that she didn't have it in her to say more that might be hurtful, either.

Then, before she could come up with anything,

a crash sounded from upstairs that drew both their attention. They got up from the table and climbed the stairs to investigate.

The picture of her late grandfather and his tractor that she'd rehung had fallen again. Apparently, the frame had been too damaged to maintain its hold. And this time when it had fallen, it had broken completely apart, the slivers of shattered glass resting on top of the photo itself.

And there it was, a fresh reminder of what Micah had most recently wreaked on her life, on her family.

She bent over and lifted the picture, careful not to disturb the broken glass, and realized that this day had gotten the best of her, that there just wasn't any more she could take.

"I'm not really hungry. I think I'll just go to bed."

"Aw, Lexie...please..."

"Good night," she answered unwaveringly before she took the picture and left him standing on the landing.

He was still there when she reached the guest room.

She could feel his eyes on her, but she didn't let that stop her as she went into the room and nudged the door closed behind her.

Things were the way they were.
And nothing could change them.
Or the way she felt about Micah because of it.

Chapter Three

"Hey, Big Ben," Micah said affectionately to his grandfather early Sunday morning.

The Camden family farmhouse—a three-story sky blue structure with an elaborate wraparound porch—was where he'd been staying with his grandfather since he'd left the Marines.

He'd searched inside for his grandfather at first, but with no answer to his calls for the elderly man, he'd gone out the back door. The shed was the likeliest place for Ben Camden to be on the only day of the week that he didn't work. And that was where Micah found him.

"Mornin'," Ben greeted, glancing up from his worktable.

He was six feet tall and, at seventy-nine, had lost a lot of the bulk he'd had in his youth. He was now less muscular and more wiry, and all four of his grandsons were inches taller than him. But they still sometimes used the nickname they'd given him when they were kids, whenever they didn't call him Pops.

"Didn't expect to see you," Ben continued. "Would have waited to have breakfast if I'da known you were comin'. I could still whip you up some eggs, though. How 'bout it?"

"Nah, thanks. I came to ask a favor and then I have to get back—that tree removal service got everything done yesterday but left one hell of a mess on the ground between the two houses. I want to clean that up."

"Get more done with a good breakfast in your belly," his grandfather said, repeating the truism he'd said a million times before. Micah couldn't help but smile at the familiar words that—like his grandfather's other sayings—had formed such an irreplaceable part of his childhood.

Micah had only been three years old, the triplets barely two, when their father was killed and they'd moved with their mother to the farm. Ben had helped to raise his grandsons after that, and he'd actually been a better cook and more of a nurturer than their mother had been—and not just because he was the one who'd prepared most of their family meals. It was no surprise that he still wanted to feed Micah—and his brothers—whenever he had the chance.

And since Micah thought Ben might be missing his company, he decided to take the time to spend with him before getting back.

"Yeah, okay, maybe a couple of eggs," Micah conceded.

"And toast and the sausage I ground and made yesterday—it fried up great for my breakfast. You're gonna love it."

"No doubt," Micah said with a laugh as his grandfather led the way back to the house.

As they worked together to make the breakfast that Ben had decided to share in, he nodded toward the mangled picture frame that Micah had left on the counter when he'd come through looking for Ben. "That the favor?"

"Yeah," Micah confirmed. "Had a picture in it of Morey Parker with a new tractor. The tree crash knocked it off the wall—I saw it when I first went through the house and left it on the floor because it didn't look like it could stand hanging up again. But Lexie must have tried when she got there and last night it fell again and really broke. I was wondering if maybe you could fix it, repaint it? You're good at that stuff."

Ben left the sausages frying and took a closer look at the frame, then returned to the stove. "I think I can do that. Seems like a drop in the bucket of what's goin' on over there, though…"

"Yeah, it is," Micah confirmed. "But I kind of had the feeling it was the straw that broke the camel's back with Lexie last night and…I don't know… I'm hoping it might make a difference somehow…"

"Things not goin' well with her?"

Micah had never confessed his misdeed to his mother or grandfather. It had never come up. Lexie's father's discovery that she and Jason were up to no good had gotten a lot more attention in town, and Micah's part in what led to that discovery had not been widely discussed.

If his mother ever had any inkling, she hadn't said anything. But things with Ben had been different than things between Raina and her sons.

Ben had always been careful not to step on his daughter-in-law's toes, not to contradict her parenting and certainly not to question her authority over her sons.

But in his own way, he had tried to subtly impart lessons without ever overtly reprimanding them. He had given little talks about remembering other people had feelings. About thinking before acting. About making good choices.

He and Micah had never openly discussed what had happened with Lexie. But Micah *had* heard all those kindly-given lectures for the nth time after the incident, so he assumed his grandfather was at least partially aware that he'd played a role in what occurred.

At any rate, he knew that Micah's friendship with Lexie and Jason had ended then. And given that Ben also knew that Micah's forklift delivery had caused the damage to the Parker property now, it made sense that he'd assume there might be some bumps in the road of Lexie's return to Merritt.

"No, things are not going well with her," Micah admitted, seeing no reason to deny it.

"And you're hopin' a fixed picture frame is gonna help," Ben said, his tone making it clear that he thought Micah was barking up the wrong tree.

"Hell, I'm hoping *anything* will help, no matter how small. Plus, Morey was Gertie's husband. I don't want her coming home when she gets well and finding one of his pictures without a frame. And just in case the frame has some meaning... Well, I'm glad you can put it back together."

"I'll get right on it."

"Thanks."

"How's Gertie doin'?" Ben asked as they sat down to eat.

"Okay. Good. I just wish she hadn't gotten hurt at all."

The elderly man nodded his understanding. "Accidents happen, though. This one's not your fault."

Micah laughed slightly. "Maybe it's not my fault but I *am* accountable."

Another sage nod of the head. "Good that you recognize that. I'm proud of you. Of the man you are now."

Micah could acknowledge that only with a brief raise of his chin. The sentimentality embarrassed him. But he still liked hearing it and hoped that it was true.

"I think if you give little Lexie a chance, she'll come around," Ben said then. "Just give it some time."

Micah raised his chin in acknowledgment again, even though he wasn't convinced Ben was right about that.

But somehow his grandfather's words helped.

And he'd needed some help.

Because after last night, he'd been pretty discouraged and worried that maybe there was just no hope of reaching even civil ground with Lexie.

"Oh, you look so much better than you did yesterday!" Lexie exclaimed with relief when she first saw her grandmother on Sunday morning.

Gertrude Parker was dressed in a bright pink sweat suit. Her curly close-cropped, more-salt-than-pepper-colored hair was combed. And she was sitting in a wheelchair, her casted leg braced straight out in front of her.

"I thought you'd still be in bed," Lexie said, wondering if maybe that's where her grandmother *should* be.

"Hate lyin' around in a bed," the elderly woman said with her usual spirit.

Lexie knew better than to argue once Gertie had made up her mind about something, but she did look to Mary to ask, "Is it all right that she's up and dressed?"

"Doctor Joan says whatever she feels like she can do is all right for her to do—as long as she doesn't put any weight on the leg and keeps it elevated."

Glancing back to her grandmother, Lexie said, "How *do* you feel?"

"Good," Gertie answered unequivocally.

It was Mary who went on, "Doctor Joan and her nurse, Louise, were here early, and Louise is going to come every morning to help get Gertie up and dressed. And she's only had half a pain pill."

"Is that enough?"

"It is," Gertie insisted. "They were making me too woozy and the pain isn't that bad to start with." She had been raised by a no-nonsense German father amid four older brothers who had treated her like one of the boys. There was very little about the older woman that succumbed to weakness.

"Doctor Joan said she should judge her pain level and whether or not she needs the pills, and rest if she gets tired," Mary put in. "But Doctor Joan also says that she has forty-year-old patients who aren't doing as well as Gert is."

The color in Gertie's cheeks today helped Lexie actually believe the report of her grandmother doing well. It also helped her to believe that Gertie would be all right.

"I'm so relieved that you're okay," she said, relaxing enough to sit in the rocking chair near her grandmother's wheelchair.

"You look better than you did yesterday, too," Gertie said then.

Lexie laughed. "Did I look bad yesterday?"

"You looked tired and so on edge that I thought you might jump right out of your skin," her grandmother described.

"I *was* tired and on edge. It was a long trip that I started in the middle of the night and I was worried about you."

Gertie waved away her concern. "It'll take more than a broken bone to do me in, honey."

Lexie didn't want to think about anything ever *doing her in*.

"Are you ready for waffles yet, Gert? Maybe Lexie will have them with us…" Mary said then.

"You guys haven't had breakfast yet?" Lexie asked in some surprise. With all they'd accomplished already today, it seemed as if they must have been up for quite a while.

"We had coffee and toast," Mary answered. "Neither of us were up yet when Doctor Joan and Louise rang the doorbell this morning. I made the coffee for us all, Doctor Joan made Gert have a few bites of toast to make sure her stomach would accept food and they didn't leave until a few minutes ago."

"We'd just decided waffles might be a nice Sunday breakfast when you got here," Gertie added. "Will you eat with us?"

As tired as Lexie had been the night before, she'd still had some trouble falling asleep. She'd gone from being overwhelmed and aggravated by Micah and telling him off in her head, to picturing him in her mind and—for no reason she could fathom—recalling how handsome he'd grown up to be. The switch from aggravation to attraction was a phenomenon she'd found disturbing.

When she'd finally fallen asleep, though, she'd slept so soundly that at nine thirty, when she'd woken up, she hadn't even remembered the alarm on her phone sounding or her having turned it off—which she must have done because she was sure she'd set it.

At that point, she'd jumped out of bed, disgusted with herself for not getting to Gertie at the crack of dawn. With no thought other than seeing her grandmother as soon as possible, she'd thrown on the yoga pants and T-shirt she'd worn briefly after her shower the night before, swiped a brush through her hair and refused to add to the delay by applying any makeup.

Then she'd gone downstairs, thrilled to find only a note from Micah, snatched her grandmother's car keys from the hook near the front door and hurried out to the car—all without so much as a drink of water or a bite to eat.

And since she'd also forgone most of her dinner the night before, she was starving.

"Waffles sound great," she said.

"Then waffles it is," Mary responded enthusiastically.

"Can I help?" Lexie offered.

"You just sit and visit with Gertie," her cousin insisted, leaving them alone in the apartment's living room.

Her grandmother reached over the wheelchair's armrest and squeezed Lexie's knee. "I'm so glad you're home. And to stay!" the older woman rejoiced.

"I'm so glad you're glad," Lexie responded.

"But not glad yourself to be back in Merritt?" Gertie asked, obviously trying to interpret Lexie's uncertain tone. "I thought that was what you wanted."

"It was. It is. I *am* glad to be back. I don't ever want to leave again."

"But?" Gertie prompted.

But Lexie was having feelings that confused her.

"It's nothing really. Everything is all just so... not how I thought it would be," she said, trying to sort through her own emotions. "I thought I'd come back to find everything still the way it was— home, you know? I thought it would wrap around me like a big comfy blanket, and I'd be able to take a deep breath for the first time in a long time, and figure out my future. Instead—" she gave a humorless laugh "—I don't know what kind of shape the little house is in or how much work it'll need to get it to where I can live in it—"

"Micah is going to take care of it."

Lexie didn't comment on that. "Plus, this is the first time in my life I've been here without Jason." Lexie struggled for the words to explain what she was having trouble grasping herself. "I hadn't thought about it being weird, but for some reason it is. And on the flip side, there's *so much Micah*..."

"Do you want Jason back?" Gertie asked, probing while still clearly trying to keep her voice neutral.

Lexie answered with another humorless chuckle. "No. It isn't that. It *really* isn't. And this *is* where I want to be, where I've wanted to be for years now. But up until the last few months, whenever I've pictured coming home, I've also pictured coming home with Jason for a future that we could both dig into. Since the divorce, that picture changed and got sort of off-kilter, but I thought once I hit Merritt, I'd regain some balance—"

"Instead, you came home to chaos and commotion and upheaval. And that's the last thing you need right now," her grandmother summed up for her.

"Yeah," Lexie agreed wistfully before switching to a snarl and repeating, *"And there's so much Micah..."*

"But Micah is a good thing because he's going to get us out of the chaos and commotion and upheaval."

That didn't make Lexie laugh—humorlessly or otherwise. Especially after hearing the admiration with which her grandmother kept referring to Micah.

"How much of a mess are we in at the farm?" Gertie asked then.

"There's definitely a mess," Lexie said, hedging. She was unsure to what extent she should burden her ailing grandmother.

"How much?" Gertie demanded.

The older woman had never been a shrinking violet or the kind of person who liked being kept in the dark, so Lexie decided not to spare her. "I've only seen your house—I haven't been in the little house yet, though Micah left a note this morning asking me to meet him at the house later today so he could show me things there. But your house is... Well, I suppose it could have been worse..."

Lexie went on to tell her grandmother about that portion of the damage to the farm.

"The tree is already gone, though," she ended on a more positive note. "There was a crew there yesterday that took care of it."

"That was Micah's doing," Gertie said, again with clear affection for Lexie's former friend. "I heard him making arrangements before I went into surgery."

"It's *all* been Micah's doing," Lexie muttered, unwilling to forget that he bore responsibility for the situation in the first place.

"Don't blame Micah," Gertie said firmly.

"It's his fault."

"It's *not* his fault. This was an accident and he didn't have anything to do with it—"

"It was *his* forklift being delivered."

"But not him unloading it—it was the deliveryman who lost control," Gertie pointed out. "And accidents happen. I knew that old tree was unstable—the trunk was rotted out. I had it looked at in the fall and the tree man said a good wind could blow it over. But I didn't want to be bothered with it right then. I thought it could make it to this summer. I shouldn't have waited. It's as much—or more—my fault for putting off what I should have had done."

Lexie hadn't known that. But still she said, "The tree *didn't* just fall down, though. Micah's wayward forklift *knocked* it down."

"And now poor Micah is wracked with guilt."

Poor Micah...

Lexie couldn't say his name without scorn and her grandmother couldn't seem to say it without fondness. Why was that? she wondered.

"You've always been so easy on him—I never understood that," Lexie admitted.

When Micah had betrayed his friendship with her and Jason, Gertie couldn't have been more sympathetic to Lexie. Gertie had battled with her son over his punishments, fought against him exiling her to boarding school, fought against him ruining her senior year. She'd supported Lexie, championed her. She'd unwaveringly been in Lexie's corner.

But she also hadn't condemned Micah.

She hadn't defended him, she hadn't broached the subject of him with Lexie or advised forgiveness or even compassion, nor had she made any attempts to reconcile their friendship.

But it had seemed as if she felt protective of Micah, too—not just of Lexie.

And when Lexie had said outright that she didn't want her grandmother having anything to do with him, Gertie's response had been, *Oh, honey, I can't do that. But it doesn't mean that what he did was right. It wasn't.*

She *had* made sure to keep Micah far from Lexie. And given that Gertie had been her only advocate, Lexie hadn't been left with much choice but to ignore that Gertie hadn't shunned Micah.

"I never understood why you kept having anything to do with him—from years ago and right up until now," Lexie admitted.

"Well, it just wasn't so cut and dry, honey. He and Jason and Jill had been at the farm with you from when you were little bitty kids. I'd been baking the bunch of you cookies and putting Band-Aids on your boo-boos and helping you with your school projects and listening to your stories and your tall tales and your gripes—you were *all* like my grandkids."

Lexie begrudgingly conceded to that. Gertie *had* always grandmothered the four of them and Jason, Micah and Jill had frequently called her *Gram* the same way Lexie did.

"And if you'll recall," Gertie went on, "when everything happened with you years ago, Micah was a stock boy at the general store. He and I had been working together for months. You know taking a job at the store every now and then was how we got by during lean times, but when I signed up that time, they'd computerized everything and they told me I could only have the job if I could deal with that. Micah was my godsend. He helped me learn their whole system. If not for that, I wouldn't have been able to work there anymore."

"Okay, but then he kept coming around the house, too—the same way he had when he was hanging out with Jason and Jill and me—because you were letting him help you make your beer."

"He was so lost then... He was such a misguided boy..." Gertie said sympathetically. "And I knew why he did what he did to you—"

"Because he was a big jerk!"

"It was a rotten thing to do," Gertie agreed.

"And yet you still seemed to feel *sorry* for him."

"I felt sorrier for you," her grandmother reminded. "But I knew what was going on with him, too. I'd watched it for so long..." Gertie shook her head sadly.

"Watched what? All his competing with Jason?" Lexie asked. "Always trying to one-up him, to get under Jason's skin? Calling us *Mom and Dad* because we were a couple and he thought that was so stupid? I don't know what there was about any of that to feel sorry for."

"He was just so much a bull in a china shop," Gertie said. "But I knew he wasn't a bad boy— even when he caused all hell to break loose for you, it was only another blockhead move he made because he was stumbling around with no idea how to move toward what he really wanted. And he paid for it, too—he lost all his friends in one fell swoop because Jill was on your side of it all and wouldn't have anything to do with him, either. So yes, I did feel sorry for him, too, and yes, I did let him follow me around—and I gave him a job or two when I was making beer because he needed somewhere to go, something to do so he didn't get into more trouble. But he grew up, he went off, he served his country. He became the good man I thought he could be. So even though you might not have liked it then or understood it, I won't apologize for not shutting him out. It didn't make what he did any less wrong. I just thought he needed a little grace from somebody."

"Or maybe—when it comes to him—you were blind then and you're blind now," Lexie said with a sigh.

Gertie merely smiled a knowing smile. "I want you to play nice with him," her grandmother commanded.

"I'm not going to play with him at all."

Lexie didn't know why that had come out sounding salacious. She just hoped her grandmother hadn't noticed.

"I want you to *work* nice with him, then," Gertie amended. "Truth to tell, our insurance coverage on the houses isn't great, honey. I haven't been smart about keeping up on increasing it the way I should have—it's like the tree. I put it off. I know the insurance money won't cover everything. But Micah has promised to bring in help with the reconstruction and to do what he can of the job himself, too, to get it all done with as little burden on me as possible. So for your sake and for mine, you have to be nice. And thankful." Gertie sighed. "And maybe give him just a little benefit of the doubt?" she said hopefully.

"There's no doubt that he did what he did, or that what came out of it, came out of it," Lexie said flatly.

"But so much time has passed… Maybe you could work on letting go? I think it would do you a world of good—carrying a grudge is a heavy load. And especially now, with both of you living here again, and him with his business in the barn, right out our back doors… Maybe it's time to just bury the hatchet? It's important to me. It's two of my own at odds, and I want it to stop. I want things to be *okay*. I'm an old lady and I don't like fighting. I don't want to be in the middle of it anymore."

Lexie *could* understand that point of view.

"I'll try not to be unpleasant," she finally conceded.

"It isn't much but I'll take it!" Gertie said victoriously.

It may have seemed to Gertie like a small concession, but as Mary informed them that the waffles were ready, Lexie could only hope that she could pull it off. After all, she hadn't even been able to make it through dinner with him last night. And she couldn't really say she'd been pleasant at any point since he'd shown up at the airport in Billings yesterday.

Still, for her grandmother's sake, she vowed she would try harder.

And hope that before too long she could regain some distance from Micah Camden.

Lexie stayed at Mary's apartment until after three o'clock when the older women decided they needed naps.

On her way out, Lexie mentioned coming back later but Gertie nixed that idea. She let Lexie know that she didn't expect—or want—Lexie to play nursemaid. Mary and the visiting nurse had that covered. Instead, while she wanted Lexie to visit, she mostly wanted her to focus on dealing with the property damage and getting settled again in Merritt.

Besides, she'd been informed that the ladies' poker group that Gertie and Mary belonged to was bringing dinner over tonight, and if Gertie was up to it, they'd be playing a few hands.

So rather than making plans to return that evening, Lexie had said she'd be back in the morning.

The farmhouse was still empty when she got home. Micah had said in his note that he needed to be at the brewery this afternoon, but that he'd meet her at the big house at five o'clock. He'd warned her not to go to the little house without him because it was more unstable than Gertie's place and needed to be carefully navigated to avoid getting hurt.

Mary and Gertie had insisted on giving her portions of the over-abundance of casseroles they'd already been given by friends and neighbors, so the first thing Lexie did was take the paper bag full of food to unload into the refrigerator.

Then, with some time on her hands—and because it seemed as if she would be in the guest room indefinitely—Lexie went upstairs and unpacked her suitcases.

She finished that at about four o'clock, and decided to use the hour until Micah's return to do what she would have done if she hadn't been in such a rush to get out this morning—she took a long, leisurely shower and shampooed her hair.

When she was finished, she blow-dried her hair using a large round brush that left the long strands smooth and sleek. It was more trouble than she usually went to but she felt an unexplained urge to put more care into her appearance.

Then she went to choose what to wear and found herself wondering if it might be time for her to start wearing her post-divorce clothes.

Over the years, her personal style had continued in the vein of the tomboy-wear of her youth.

Given the bare-bones lifestyle she and Jason had lived, it had just made sense. Everything she'd owned—and there wasn't much of it—had been more practical and functional than fashionable, frilly or fancy. It all had to be easy to pack, easy to wash and dry, and sturdy enough not to need frequent replacement.

The fact that almost every job she'd had over the years had come with a uniform had helped keep her personal things minimalistic.

The post-divorce wardrobe was a different story.

It hadn't been her idea but Lily's—her boss in Alaska who had become a friend. Lily had decreed that while Jason had allotted himself a new life, Lexie should at least have some new clothes that didn't make her look so plain and *married*—something Lily had said with distaste.

Lexie hadn't realized that what she'd been wearing had done that, but on that particular day, when she'd been at a low point, she'd liked the idea of a new look. So she'd thrown caution to the wind with her first credit card as a single person and indulged in a shopping spree. A shopping spree with fun-loving Lily at the helm—Lily who had also given her a place to live when she'd left Jason, and let her stay that first month without contributing any money for rent or utilities since she'd spent all her money on her new look.

The shopping spree had netted Lexie three pairs

of better-fitting jeans, half a dozen new tops, two dresses and date slacks that went with three different date tops—despite her protests against the likelihood of dating anytime soon.

She'd also gone back to Lily's apartment that day with new shoes to replace her sneakers and loafers—some everyday Mary Janes, some ballet-style shoes, one pair of low heels and one pair of high.

She'd been the most uncomfortable buying the new underwear her friend had insisted on. But Lily had been even more adamant about the undies than anything. Nothing, she'd said, made a new woman more than new underwear. And so Lexie had ended up with a collection of less sensible and much lacier bras and panties.

The shopping had taken place months ago and Lexie had yet to wear any of it. Her waitress job had required a uniform supplied by the hotel restaurant that Lily managed, and on her off-hours Lexie had never felt like doing more than pulling on some sweats and hibernating until it was time for work again. And she certainly hadn't dated anyone.

But now?

Now she was in Merritt for her fresh start and the thought of those new clothes suddenly held some appeal.

As she opened her underwear drawer and looked

down at the old items on one side and the new on the other, the nearly-granny panties seemed like things only Gertie should wear. So she opted for a pair of bikini briefs.

And instead of choosing one of the old semi-sports bras she'd worn since college, she grabbed the much more feminine bra that Lily had talked her into because she'd said it didn't flatten her out so much.

She realized when she put on the underwear that it really did make her feel like a new woman, and that gave her a burst of confidence when she moved on to the closet.

It was the new things she was drawn to there, too, she discovered, telling herself that if the new underwear gave her a touch more self-assurance, why not let the new outerwear work toward that, too? Then maybe she wouldn't feel such dread over seeing Micah again. As far as she was concerned, she was facing a foe when she faced him, and it was always good to have any advantage in that situation.

So on went a pair of the new tightly fitted jeans.

With those in place, she turned her back to the full-length mirror on the inside of the closet door and craned around to look at the rear view.

Lily had said the better cut of jeans made her butt look great. Lexie had taken her word for it but now that she took her own assessment, she decided there *was* an improvement.

Next came a plain white tank top underneath a pale pink T-shirt with a wide square neckline. The double layer was a trend she'd always avoided, but now that she saw the effect, she liked it.

The fact that the T-shirts were tighter than she usually wore would take getting used to, but for some reason that snugger fit made her pull her shoulders back and let her new bra do its bit of added accentuation.

And sure enough, she felt a little surge of renewed confidence shoot through her.

"Okay…" she said to her reflection by way of approval.

Then she returned to the bathroom where she'd put her makeup in the medicine cabinet.

During one of her many at-home nights after her split from Jason, Lily had also suggested a tutorial on *not-married* makeup.

She'd been disinclined to do all Lily did—which required a full half hour of application. But after the tutorial, she had begun a routine of applying a tinted moisturizer to even out her skin tone, a powder blush, a darker eyeliner and mascara. So that was what she used now.

When she finished with that, she ran a brush through her hair one last time, returned to the closet to slip her feet into a pair of ballet shoes and allowed one more look at herself in the full-length mirror to take in the whole picture.

It *was* an improvement but mostly, she told herself, it meant she didn't look tired or stressed out.

And that made the new clothes and attention to makeup the right choices, she concluded. Tired and stressed out were not the impressions she wanted to give to anyone. Rested, healthy, strong, in control and ready, willing and able to take on the next chapter of her life—that was what she wanted anyone looking at her to think.

And if Micah was among those anyones?

She hadn't liked the way she'd ended the previous evening with him.

She'd come across as frazzled. Overwrought. Maybe even fragile. Fleeing from him.

And apparently looking tired on top of it.

That put her at a disadvantage.

If she had to again be face-to-face with him, then she at least wanted to look her best. She wanted to look as if she'd risen above all the blows in her life—the one he'd dealt and the ones Jason had. As if she was moving on. From them and from their actions. And even if Jason wasn't there to see the evidence of that, Micah was.

So go ahead and take a good look, she said silently. *You both may have knocked me down, but I'm getting back up!*

* * *

Micah still wasn't there when Lexie went downstairs even though it was past five o'clock.

She made her way through the smashed-up kitchen, glancing into the sunroom to the right—the room Micah had said he'd be living out of.

Sure enough, the foldout couch was made up with sheets, blanket and pillows, all in military precision neatness.

"Are you here?" she called out, just in case he was somewhere out of sight.

There was no answer and curiosity pushed her close enough to see more of the space.

There was a duffel bag peeking from behind a chair, but it was so meticulously placed there that it was barely visible. Other than that and the sheets on the bed, there were no signs that anyone was living here. It was as orderly as her grandmother kept it.

"So you're better at housekeeping than your old friend, my ex," she muttered as she retraced her steps to go to the kitchen sink and the window above it.

The barn was about a hundred feet from the rear of the house—easily visible from either Gertie's place or the kitchen of the little house.

The big barn doors were open wide and standing just inside of them was Micah and another man. Micah was facing out, as if he was about to make his exit, the other man was in profile and holding a clipboard he was referring to as he talked.

"Okay, it's almost five thirty..." Lexie said. "Will you live up to what Gram thinks of you or will you prove me right? Because I think you'll put yourself and your own interests before ours—like always..."

There was no possibility that he could have heard her utterance, but as if he had, he shot a glance at the big house.

So you know this is where you're supposed to be...

But then he continued talking to the other man.

And she continued watching him.

She wondered if he'd been clean-shaven earlier and his beard had grown back through the day, or if the scruff that shadowed that angular face was a holdover from the day before.

Either way, she wished he were clean-shaven.

If he were, maybe he would look more like he had when they were kids. When she'd recognized that he was boyishly cute but it hadn't done anything for her.

Not that the way he looked now did anything for her. Or to her.

She just kept *noticing* how hot he was now, and she didn't want to. His rugged masculinity almost made him seem like a different person and she didn't want to think of him as a different person. He was who he was and she didn't want any awareness of that fact to fade.

Micah had on what appeared to be military issue cargo pants and a gray hoodie emblazoned with United States Marines and the Marine insignia.

The hoodie didn't fit as tightly as the T-shirt he'd had on the previous day, and while Lexie didn't want to acknowledge it, she still had the image of that T-shirt's knit stretched tight across impressively well-developed pectorals, hugging a narrow waist and a perfectly flat stomach. The T-shirt had also better framed the equally well-developed neck that Lexie didn't recall him having when they'd known each other before. Plus, there was the T-shirt's short sleeves that had been stretched taut around massively muscled biceps.

Not that she *preferred* one view over the other, she told herself, but she did find herself mentally picturing what was under that sweatshirt.

And wondering if, once he was inside, he might take it off.

If he actually did leave the brewery…

"He's not going to come," she said with some derision to remind herself to keep her focus.

Micah did take a step more out the door but just then a third man rushed up to him to hand Micah a small vial that Micah drank out of.

Whatever he'd tasted made him recoil and shake his head as he handed the vial back to the third man.

He again glanced toward the house but he still stayed where he was as he spoke with the third man.

"You're gonna go back in there and leave me hanging," Lexie said. "Better listen to me, Gram, because when it comes to him you're—"

Not wrong?

Because just then Micah held up both hands to cut off the other men. From what Lexie could tell, Micah seemed to give them instructions—but then he left them behind to head for the house.

"Okay, maybe this time he's doing what he said he would. But just wait..." she muttered, convinced that like her ex-husband, like the Micah of old, ultimately his own interests would win out.

"I'm sorry I'm late," he said as he came in the back door. "Something went wrong with the flavoring of one of my tester batches of beer. We've been trying to figure out why but it'll wait. My hands are sticky. Let me wash up and we can get going."

So he'd left a problem in order to keep his word to her?

He really must be running on high-octane guilt, Lexie thought, certain this was a fluke.

She didn't say anything. She just moved to the side of the sink to free the way for him.

He pushed the sweatshirt's sleeves up, revealing massive wrists and forearms. Then he turned on the water and lathered hands that she didn't remember being so big, either. Big, strong, capable-looking hands that, for some reason, she couldn't stop looking at.

What could possibly be sexy about hands or washing them? she asked herself.

And yet it somehow struck her that way.

"How's Gertie today?" he asked as he rinsed the lather and took a sheet of paper towel to dry off.

Lexie forcibly snapped herself out of her reverie. "Gram is good—she said you called this morning to check on her so you should know that."

"Yeah, but she'll always say that. You have to have eyes on her to know for sure."

That was true. "She's well enough to try to play a little poker with the ladies tonight."

That made him smile and Lexie realized it was the first time she'd seen him do that since the old days.

His smile was still a little lopsided—the left corner of his mouth quirked up just a fraction higher than the right. It had always made his smile seem cocky but now that seemed sexy, too, and she wondered what was wrong with her to keep thinking of him that way.

"Ah, Gertie," he breathed with a small laugh. "She's one of kind."

There was no disputing that, either.

Finished with the paper towel, he tossed it in the trash. "So what do you say? Are you ready to see the little house?"

"Sure," she answered.

"I have to warn you, there's more damage there than here. And I spent what time I could yesterday cleaning up this house because I knew you and I would be using it. The little house hasn't been touched—except for the tarps I put up to keep out the elements. What I'm saying is that it might be harder on you to see—especially since you lived there with your folks. So brace yourself."

"I'm sure I'll be fine," she said, dismissing his concern.

In her mind, she could see her grandmother shaking a disapproving head at her for her curt tone, reminding her that she'd promised not to be unpleasant.

Mixed with that was her conscience reminding her that Micah's own attitude, even in the face of her snottiness, held no hostility or even impatience. Not even now, when he could easily have been out of sorts over abandoning a business problem to deal with her.

She wasn't forgiving him, but at this point, keeping up a bad attitude was beginning to seem petty. So not only to keep her promise to her grandmother but also for her own sake, Lexie took a deep breath and swore to do better.

"Shall we go?" Micah asked.

"Sure," she repeated, this time without the snark.

They went out the front door of the big house, crossed the yard and entered the front door of the little house.

Micah was right about there being more damage—so much more than Lexie had expected, despite his warning.

Almost half of the house where she'd grown up was rubble.

The floorplan of the little house was similar to Gertie's but in reverse. So, like the big house, the tree had taken out the side wall of the kitchen downstairs and the master bedroom upstairs, only it had destroyed more of both.

In the kitchen, no cupboards or appliances had survived, and neither had the kitchen table around which Lexie had had so many meals with her parents. The antique cupboard her mother had loved was just kindling. The kitchen sink had been ripped away, the pipes to it left poking out of the wall.

Micah explained that the plumbing exposure and the dangling electrical wires from the destroyed light fixture had caused the building inspector to order the water and power shut off.

There were also holes in the kitchen floor. A missed step could drop her into the root cellar.

Getting upstairs was more treacherous, too, because some of the stairs had been broken. Once they got to the second level, Lexie found that nearly the entire master bedroom and bath were gone, and that the bed and dressers her parents had used were demolished.

"The good news is that you'll get a remodel and an update," Micah said after the tour as they returned to Gertie's house.

It was on the tip of her tongue to lash out at him, to say that what had comforted her through her divorce was the thought of coming home to what was familiar, what was comfortable. She didn't want new and updated—she wanted her home back.

But she put conscious effort into *not* saying that, told herself firmly that moving forward was better than crying over spilt milk and replied, "Gram said something about you getting people to help do the work…"

"I belong to a Vets Helping Vets group in Billings. It's nothing formal, just some guys like me who got out in one piece. We do what we can for each other and for older or injured vets who might need a hand here and there."

That sounded commendable. In an attempt to be less caustic, she said, "That's really nice."

He didn't acknowledge the praise. He just went

on, "A lot of the guys in the group work construction, so I put out the word. I've already had a few callbacks—they're getting a crew together. Plus, there are a couple of guys who'll come on their own and do what they can in their off-hours. The biggest problem is time. They all have jobs and lives, so it won't be a matter of starting things here and working until they're done. It'll be a couple days work, then they'll be gone, then a couple more days work—"

"That could take forever," Lexie said, alarmed by the thought, the edge back in her tone.

"It won't be quick," Micah confirmed, still calm, not reacting to her cutting tenor. "Construction is a pain and I'm not going to lie to you—it'll be dragged out some. But I'll do everything I can to make it as easy as possible on you—and on Gertie when we can get her back here. And it'll be worth it in the end. The labor will all be free, we'll have a good-sized crew sometimes that'll make a big dent when they *are* here. Anybody who has a day they can spare even without the rest of the guys will come, and I'll do what I can… We'll get it all done," he assured her.

Lexie just sighed in frustration. She genuinely wanted to be wrong about him when it came to this, because she and her grandmother had no recourse but to count on him and his Vets Helping Vets. But it was clearly not going to be a picnic.

But because she thought she should give him a little credit for tearing himself away from his business to give her the tour, she said, "People have been bringing food to Mary and Gertie—more than they can fit in the fridge or freezer—so they sent a bunch of it home with me. If you want to fix something to eat and get back to work—"

They'd reached the front door of the big house by then and he held it open for her. "Why don't we both eat and then I'll go back?"

That shouldn't have been the answer she wanted to hear, and yet somehow it was.

Maybe she just hadn't been looking forward to eating alone...

"Okay," she agreed, having no clue why she was so all over the place when it came to him.

They decided to microwave bowls of shepherd's pie for dinner. As they sat together at the kitchen table for the second evening in a row, Micah said, "So the grand plan was for you and Jason to go to college to get teaching degrees. Then you were going to take a year to travel, come back here, settle down and teach. You figured you could save up during the school year and travel every summer during you time off," he said, surprising her with his clear memory of what she and Jason had talked about when they'd all been friends.

"Best laid plans..." she said under her breath.

"I heard through the grapevine—well, from my

brothers—that Jason got antsy and quit college during the first semester, and that after your folks were killed in that accident, you put off your second year. That surprised me."

"I was so scattered, so sad, I couldn't concentrate on school. And I just… I wanted to get away from it all. Escape. It was Jason's idea that I drop out, too, that we take off, and all of a sudden being practical appealed to me less than…just escaping…" she explained.

"Did you go to Europe the way you'd planned?"

"We did. Backpacking, camping or staying in hostels. We didn't have enough money saved to travel straight through, so instead we'd get whatever jobs we could, save and then move on to the next place when money allowed." She paused, then said, "But Gram must have told you—"

He cut her off with a shake of his head. "I've kept up with Gertie, she's kept up with me—we've talked beer until we're both blue in the face over the years—but we haven't talked about you. That's sort of been an off-limits subject since days of old. So I honestly don't know what you've been up to."

Lexie wondered if that was the truth, but ultimately decided to accept it. Gertie hadn't spoken one word to her about Micah, so it didn't seem far-fetched that her grandmother hadn't kept him informed about her, either.

"Okay," she allowed.

"Did you spend more than one year in Europe?"

"Thirteen months."

"And then? Did you get back to college and get your teaching degrees?"

"Oh, no. Neither of us had any more to do with college. There's no teaching degree for me to fall back on," she said with regret.

"Did you get into some other career?"

"Career?" she said with a disheartened laugh. "No. I've done a million different things, but nothing that felt like it was part of an actual career path."

"So how did it happen that you didn't follow the plan?" he asked.

"The *plan*…" Lexie said. "To get married but delay taking on responsibility… Jason said we'd spent our whole life here and would end up here, but we should take just a little break in between to see what else was out there. And I thought that sounded like fun. An adventure."

"Was it?"

"At first. For a while. The trouble was, once we were *out there*, Jason never reached a point where he wanted to come back and take on the responsibilities we'd postponed—a regular job that he couldn't quit on a whim, a mortgage that he claimed would mean something *owned us*… He just never got to where he wanted to settle down. So instead of traveling for a year, then coming home, it's been all about moving around, finding whatever jobs we could get, staying a while, then moving on and doing it all over again."

Micah didn't comment on that. "What all have you done for work?" he asked before he took a bite of the meat-and-vegetable-laden casserole.

"I've been a nanny. I've worked in day care. I've worked in nursing homes. I've waited tables. I've worked in restaurant kitchens and bakeries. I've cleaned hotel rooms and worked the front desk. I've worked retail and sold everything from surfboards to eyeglasses. I've checked out groceries and worked in factories. I've cleaned stadium seats… Just to name a few…"

"That's more than a few," Micah marveled.

"And now I don't know what I'm going to do," Lexie admitted.

She felt as if she'd revealed more than she'd intended. Then he said, "And even though that's how it's been for years—going someplace and just finding a job when you got there—it's bothering you that that's how it is coming home."

It wasn't a question. He was definitely seeing more than she wanted him to.

She took a bite of shepherd's pie to stall.

"You could go back to college now, get your teaching degree," he suggested.

"I thought about that but I've kind of come to

a point where I want to be in a position to start thinking about having kids of my own, not putting that off to teach other people's kids."

And why had she confessed *that* to him?

"I can understand that. That's part of why I left the Marines—to get started on the future I saw for myself. I put it off long enough to serve, but now I want to get to it."

"The brewery," she guessed.

"The brewery. And coming back here to live so I could start a family one day."

"You?" she said with a real laugh. "Mr. Too-Cool? You never wanted a steady girlfriend. You always gave Jason and me a hard time about being stuck with each other forever. You told us we should be playing the field. Now *you* want a *family*?"

He didn't seem willing to look her in the eye. "I was a kid," he protested. Then he did raise his striking blue eyes to hers to say, "Besides, *that's* more normal than sticking for life to the person you started dating when you were thirteen. *Now* I'm the right age to start thinking about finding a partner for life."

And now they were talking the way they had when they'd been friends—teasing, goading, debating, not walking on eggshells…

"Okay, yes, marrying my middle school boyfriend didn't go well—I can't argue with that," she conceded.

"I'm just saying that I can see why you don't want to go to college now," he backtracked. "So what *are* you thinking about doing?"

"I don't have the slightest idea," she said with a sigh. "But I'd like it not to be just answering an ad or a help-wanted sign in a window."

"So you have to figure out what you *want* to do."

She took a deep breath and breathed it out hard. "Yeah," she said without enthusiasm.

His smile then was compassionate but also tinged with devilishness as he quoted something she'd said frequently in the past, "Make a list."

"Of what I want to be when I grow up?" she said facetiously.

"How about of all the jobs you've had, which ones you liked the most, which you liked the least and what you might want to turn into a *career*."

That sounded so much like something she would have said to him years ago that it made her laugh again.

"Simple as that?" she said.

"Hey, it's a place to start," he countered as he finished his meal.

That was another thing she'd said to him in the past when giving similar advice.

"I'll spend tonight looking for paper and a pencil while you go to work," she said glibly, thinking it was time to let him get to that. Especially when she realized, somewhat guiltily, that she was actually beginning to enjoy talking to him.

"Over there—I saw paper and pencils when I put that drawer back yesterday," he responded as he stood to put his dishes in the dishwasher, obviously accepting her dismissal.

But he turned to her again when he'd finished with his dishes and said, "Do you need anything else?"

She shook her head. "Go!"

"I'm just out in the barn. Holler if you need anything."

"I won't need anything," she promised.

He nodded and exited without another word, leaving her to her own devices.

Lexie remained at the kitchen table, digesting the fact that she felt a little sorry to see him go, that for a few minutes it had actually felt good to talk to him the way they had when they were kids.

And more than that, she was actually considering following his advice about making a list.

She got up, went to the drawer he'd indicated and took out paper and a pencil.

But not without first glancing through the window over the sink to make sure he really was on his way to the barn so he wouldn't be able to see that she was taking his suggestion.

And in the process—before she reminded herself to look away—she got a gander of a backside that was almost as good as the front.

Chapter Four

Lexie was at Mary's apartment early enough on Monday morning to sit in on Gertie's visit with the local doctor.

To Lexie's relief, Doctor Joan was so pleased with how the older woman was fairing that she decided she could hand over daily visits to her nurse, Louise, and only do her own house calls once a week.

After the visit, Mary left to run errands and Lexie stayed with her grandmother until noon when Lexie had a lunch date scheduled with Jill Gunner—now Jill Harris—the fourth member of the friend foursome of Lexie's youth.

Lexie and Jill had always been best girlfriends and that had continued even after Lexie and Jason left Merritt. They'd kept in close contact by phone, emails and texts, and whenever Jill had been able to afford a trip, she'd either gone to stay with Lexie and Jason or met Lexie somewhere in the middle.

Jill had even planned her wedding at the hotel in Hawaii where Lexie and Jason were working at the time so they could help with all the arrangements and Lexie could be Jill's matron of honor.

But since then, they had only seen each other twice in person because in those seven years Jill had had four babies—two boys and two girls.

"I can't believe you're *finally* home—and home to *stay*," Jill said as they sat at the table in Jill's quaint country kitchen.

Jill's oldest son was in half-day kindergarten so had arrived home about the time Lexie got there. She'd helped Jill feed all four siblings lunch, then the kids had gone down for naps—though the kindergartner had insisted to Lexie that he didn't sleep, he only *rested*.

With the children tucked away, Jill had brought out tarragon chicken salad sandwiches for their lunch and settled in to chat. They covered Gertie's condition, Jill's life with her firefighter husband, Anthony, the latest on the kids and Jill's parents. Now, Jill was marveling for the third time on Lexie moving back to Merritt.

"That was waaay too long of a year," Jill added facetiously, referring to the fact that when Lexie and Jason left Merritt it was for what was meant to be a single gap year.

"Waaay too long," Lexie agreed.

"How're you doing with the divorce and everything?"

"Okay," Lexie answered, sharing with her friend much of what she'd told her grandmother about how odd it felt being back without Jason.

"It's all just kind of surreal… I thought we were a great love story. True soul mates…" she said sadly. "But somewhere along the way that changed. Well, actually I guess Jason changed. And I didn't. I don't know, maybe that was bad?"

"That you're stable and loyal? That after not putting down roots all this time, you came back to wanting stability in your life? Stability that Jason pretty obviously doesn't want? I don't think you're in the wrong here—but he really, really was."

Jill refilled their iced teas and took out a plate of cookies for their dessert. "But you didn't get to come home to much stability," she added. "How does your house look?"

Lexie filled her in on that subject, too. "Gram is convinced that *Micah* is going to fix everything," she said, once again unable to say his name without a sarcastic tone. "And all I can do is hope she's right."

"So now you and Micah are living together," her friend said.

"I wouldn't put it that way. We're under the same roof, but it's a big house and we stay out of each other's way."

"You know what I keep wondering?" Jill said mischievously.

"What?"

"If you had to marry one of them, do you ever think you would have been better off marrying Micah?"

"I think it would have been better if I hadn't gotten married a week after high school graduation at all. Plus, I should have stayed in college. Jason and I probably would have broken up like you and *your* high school sweetheart did, and then maybe I could have met and married somebody altogether new—like you did with Anthony."

"I can't argue with that," Jill said. "But if you *had* to marry one of our boys—"

Lexie laughed at the term they'd started using for Jason and Micah when they were small children.

"—would you have been better off with Micah?"

"I can't imagine how," Lexie concluded.

"He was the nicer of the two before he started being so determined to get what he wanted at any cost—so dog-eat-dog. Remember when he jumped over the church pew to walk with you behind your grandfather's casket? That was so sweet."

Her grandfather had died when they were in fourth grade. After the church service, her parents had walked on either side of Gertie to follow the coffin to the gravesite behind the church. Lexie had been left to walk alone behind them until Micah had forced his way to her side, where he'd stayed like a stoic little soldier through the burial. It had helped her more than any fourth grader could express.

Recalling that did touch a soft spot in Lexie. "Remember him looking all grown up in that suit and tie? We didn't even know he owned nice clothes," Lexie added in pure flashback to a time when she'd had only positive feelings for Micah.

"And remember how it was Micah and you who carried my books when I was on crutches with a broken foot in eighth grade?" Jill said. "You got mad at Jason for not helping out, and all he said was that he had his own books to carry."

Lexie nodded. There was no refuting the truth.

"I always liked talking to Micah better than Jason, too," Jill added. "He was by far the better listener."

Also true. And an experience that Lexie had revisited with Micah the evening before. Even though she didn't want to put any stock in it.

"And whenever you came to him with a problem, he'd always try to see if there was something he could do to help—I remember Jason saying more than once, *What do you expect me to do about it?*"

Lexie's laugh this time was wry. "Oh, yeah… When we first became a couple, he didn't say that kind of thing to me. But after we were married? That was like his mantra if I complained about anything. But don't forget that the one time I really needed Micah's help—to squash that rumor about the two of us in the barn—he just did more damage instead."

"Yeah, like I said, by that point, when he wanted something, look out! On the other hand, that's also what made him the star of the football team, the baseball team and the basketball team," Jill went on. "It was also Micah who always helped old Miss Jackson or mean Mr. Waters carry their groceries home from the store. Jason refused to do it because they were both so crotchety they never said thank-you, but that didn't stop Micah."

"It was why the manager eventually offered him a job—he said if Micah could put up with those two, he wanted him on the payroll." Still veering away from the positive column, though, Lexie added, "Maybe that was why he helped them. Maybe he figured there would ultimately be something in it for him."

"I don't think so. He never said that. And you

know he wasn't shy about bragging when he won something he'd set his sights on." Jill paused for a sip of tea. "But now it seems like he may have gone back to the way he was before he got so intense."

"I don't know about that," Lexie contended. "If I were you, I wouldn't risk running into a barn alone with him. It might cost you your marriage."

"No, seriously," Jill persisted. "It seems like he's turned into a pretty decent human being."

"Oh, no, not you!" Lexie exclaimed. "Gertie is definitely in the Micah Camden Fan Club, but I didn't think you would be, too."

"I wouldn't say that I'm a *fan*. Because of what he caused with the barn thing, you and I didn't get to have the senior year we'd planned. And my parents got worried about what I might be doing, so all of a sudden my curfew was *ten o'clock*! Not to mention that when Mark and I started dating, we were *never* allowed to be alone. You know I was as mad at Micah as you were. Well, almost."

Jill *had* completely cut him out, Lexie recalled.

Jill added, "And even before he pulled the barn stunt with you, Micah had gotten kind of full of himself. I haven't forgotten that."

"We tolerated it because we'd all been friends for so long," Lexie contributed.

"Until the barn thing. After that, I just wrote him off. When he left Merritt, I thought *good riddance*." Jill's tone went from heated to more quizzical. "But the thing is, he didn't come back as the same guy he was when he left. Now he's more like he was when we were kids. Now you just aren't going to find anyone who will say they're sorry he's around."

"Sure you will—me."

Jill laughed. "I know. But with everybody else? Not only did he come home a hero for serving his country but he's kind of become one around here, too. He actually saved the Mullen twins when they set fire to the basement playing with matches. Sara Mullen was out in the barn and he was just driving in from town and saw the smoke. He made her stay outside, ran in himself and got the kids out. Then he turned the hose on to keep the fire from spreading before the fire department could get there. He was so impressive that Anthony and the guys tried to recruit him. When they couldn't, they talked him into becoming a volunteer firefighter."

"So he did a good deed. But that doesn't mean he still wouldn't stab somebody in the back to get what he wanted," Lexie insisted.

"He just doesn't give that impression anymore, though. He's been right there with Anthony and the rest of the guys helping out with the hail damage that hit some people hard—even when it cost him time away from his brewery. I can't tell you how many things he's pitched in for when there's been a need—even at his own expense. And he's just…" Jill shrugged again. "I kept my distance when he first got back, but it's a small town and with both of us living here—"

"And with your husband and the whole fire department also apparently belonging to his fan club," Lexie put in.

"He and Anthony have definitely become friends," Jill admitted. "But anyway, I've had to sort of re-assess him. And the truth is, he's more like the boy in the suit at your grandfather's funeral than the barn guy. He's… I don't know… It's like he doesn't have anything to prove anymore. He definitely isn't full of himself like he was in high school. And I haven't seen any signs that he's only out for himself."

"Maybe there just hasn't been anything he wants badly enough to bring that side out in him yet," Lexie suggested.

"Oh, he wants that brewery to succeed," Jill said. "It's his baby and everybody knows it."

"Then that doesn't bode well for getting our houses fixed…"

"What have you seen from him so far? Would you say he's the same or different?" Jill asked.

Lexie thought about the evening before, about him leaving behind a problem at his brewery in order to keep his word to her. About him keeping her company through dinner before going back.

"Maybe he's just better at hiding things," she

said, unwilling to let down her guard any more than she already had.

"But I heard that he's been busting his butt taking care of everything over at your place since the tree…"

Lexie wanted to point out yet again that Micah was responsible for the damage—but she was tired of trying to argue that. Instead, all she said was, "But is he going to see it through to the end? Because there's a ton of work that needs to be done, and he said himself that it'll take a lot of time. That will mean a lot of time away from his own interests. Do you really think that when push comes to shove, he'll keep it up? Or do you think he'll prioritize his own stuff and leave us hanging?"

Jill shrugged, clearly not confident enough in Micah to be certain. "Maybe it's the optimist in me, but for your sake and Gertie's sake—and for his, too—I'm going to hope he really is the kind of man who won't let you down."

"I guess we'll see," Lexie said.

Something about that made Jill laugh a little wickedly. "And oh, boy, what there *is* to see now! Can you believe how that wiry kid we used to hang out with has buffed up? I mean, he always had a great face and those eyes…what I would have given to have eyes like those myself!" Jill rolled hers rapturously. "But there wasn't much muscle to him. But now… Whew, he's something to look at!"

Lexie laughed. And felt incredibly relieved. Every time her gaze got stuck on some spectacularly handsome detail of Micah, every time she discovered herself ogling him and appreciating the sight so much more than she wanted to, she'd start to worry that she might be developing some kind of involuntary attraction to him.

But hearing that her friend—who was devoted to her husband and who had only ever seen Micah as a brother—was aware of some of the same things?

That meant that anyone with eyes grasped that he'd become a fine-looking specimen of man. It wasn't only her. And it wasn't anything she had to be concerned about.

"Yeah, how unfair is it that he got better-looking with age? Drop-dead gorgeous—if we're being completely honest," she agreed with her friend.

"So you *have* noticed."

"I'd have to be blind not to," Lexie said matter-of-factly.

"Then it's probably a good thing you *aren't* a fan. Otherwise, with the two of you living in the same house, it might be asking for trouble."

"No chance of that," Lexie swore.

But considering the fact that she wasn't dreading the thought of going home to him? That she might even be looking forward to it a little?

Unfortunately, there was nothing in what Jill had said that could ease her mind about that...

* * *

"For dinner, I'm grilling bratwurst—my grandfather made it with my oat stout," Micah announced to Lexie when she arrived home a little after six o'clock.

He must have just showered because the clean scent of soap came with him and his hair was damp.

Altogether—smell plus the sight of him in jeans and a chest-hugging T-shirt—for a split second, it stopped her in her tracks as a purely primitive appreciation of him went to her head.

Or maybe she was just hungry since lunch had been hours ago.

She hung on to that thought because it made her feel better about her own reaction.

She'd stayed at Jill's long enough to say hello when Anthony got home from work, but she'd declined the invitation to spend the evening with them, telling herself that it was because she didn't want to intrude on their family time, and not because of Micah.

Standing there in her grandmother's kitchen with him, it did strike her that they seemed to have already fallen into a dinner routine. One that she should nip in the bud.

But then what? Start a new routine of trying to avoid him at mealtimes? Eat in her room so they didn't meet up in the kitchen?

That would only make this situation more awkward. The situation she'd promised her grandmother that she would attempt to make better, not worse.

She assured herself that it was not that she *wanted* to have dinner with him—she just wanted to live up to her promise to Gertie. That was the only reason she said, "Okay—I like bratwurst. But can I shower first? I'm coated in baby spit up and strained peas and melted Popsicle and some kind of fruit-in-a-pouch stuff. The mix of smells is kind of sickening. Plus, I think there's some finger paint in my hair."

He grinned.

And that just made it worse, because that grin was so disarming and lit up those damnable blue eyes of his.

"Jill's kids?" he guessed. When their paths had crossed earlier that day, Lexie had told him that she was seeing Gertie in the morning and their old friend in the afternoon.

"Four is a lot of them," she said in answer.

"Go ahead and shower. I'll get the coals nice and hot and won't put the brats on until you come down—so no hurry."

She took her time in the shower, relieved to note that Micah had left her plenty of hot water. Choosing what to wear afterward, she refused to let herself put too much effort into her clothes.

She bypassed the post-divorce things and put

on clean black yoga pants with a T-shirt. Admittedly, she'd only ever worn the T-shirt for casual-dressy occasions when she'd been married—it was a white knit crewneck with a crocheted inset across the top that raised it a notch above an everyday tee. But still, it was from the married side of the closet so she figured that gave it reduced status.

She also reapplied her makeup, reasoning again that that was merely for her own confidence.

As for her hair, she simply brushed it and left it down.

Micah was outside at the grill when she returned to the kitchen, his face still shadowed with stubble that was no thicker than it had been that morning, making her think he trimmed the stubble to keep it just the length he wanted it.

When he spotted her, he took a plate of raw bratwurst from the picnic table and put them on the grill.

While she was upstairs he'd also set the picnic table with plates, silverware and napkins, hot dog buns and spicy mustard for the brats, plus potato chips, dill pickle slices, cheese and crackers, and green olives to round out the meal.

"It's so nice today I thought we could eat outside," he told her as she went into the yard.

When the sunroom had been the patio, there had been nothing but topsoil from there to the barn. After enclosing the patio to make it the sunroom,

Gertie had laid a walkway of flagstones to the barn and planted a small patch of lawn. That was where the picnic table, bench seats and the barbecue grill were.

On the other side of the walkway, she'd installed a firepit with a small semi-circular wicker outdoor sofa that curved halfway around it.

That setup was more intimate than the picnic table so Lexie was happy to avoid it.

She offered to get drinks, and a moment later she retraced her steps into the tarped kitchen, filled two glasses with water and ice, and went out again.

"How's Gertie today?" Micah asked then.

Lexie gave him the update.

"And Jill?" he inquired afterward.

"She's good. And she's a *mom...*," Lexie mused, noting the thing she'd been marveling at all afternoon and the whole way home. "It seems so strange... Are we really old enough to have kids? And *four* of them?"

She had no idea why that made him frown for a minute before he said with some solemnity, "We're definitely old enough."

There seemed to be some underlying darkness about that subject for him, but Lexie decided to skirt around what was none of her business. "Well, anyway, she's taken to parenthood like a duck to water, and her kids are cute and funny, and I've liked Anthony since the first time I met him, so altogether I'd say they're a perfect little family."

"I don't think four kids counts as a *little* family, but perfect? Yeah, it seems that way to me, too," Micah agreed. "Good for them."

"I hope it always is," Lexie said quietly, hearing the solemnity in her own voice. The topic touched a divorce nerve with her.

Micah let the subject drop. Instead, they both breathed in some of the aromas of the cooking bratwurst. They agreed that the smell alone was great.

Then Lexie said, "I didn't know your grandfather made sausage. Does he grind his own meats and everything?"

"Oh, yeah. It's become a hobby for him. He makes all kinds but this is his first experiment adding my beer."

"How does he add beer to it? Does he inject it after it's in the casing? Or mix it with the spices? Or—"

"He won't tell me. He says he's keeping it a secret and hinting that I might not end up being the only one of us selling products through the Camden Superstores."

"So he wants to turn it into a side business?"

"Maybe."

Micah tested one of the brats and judged them cooked. He grabbed an empty plate from the picnic table, put two links on it and then moved the rest off the heat to the outer edge of the grill where they would still be kept warm. "Let's see how they are."

"Is there something unique I should taste from the beer being yours?" Lexie asked as they sat across from each other, assembled their sandwiches and filled their dishes with the other things on the table.

"I hope so," he said. "If my beers aren't unique, they won't make it. And that would be… I can't even think about it…" he said, his tone weighty for a second time.

"You have a lot riding on this," Lexie guessed.

"Nah, not a lot. Everything," he said simply.

"Everything?"

"Every penny of my own money —the money I've saved through all the years in the Marines. My grandfather turned over half his fields to me to grow hops—which means that if I fail, he'll be losing money on the land, cutting into a substantial part of his income this year. My Camden cousins in Colorado have invested in the brewery, along with putting a lot of money into an advertising campaign to launch selling Camden Microbrews exclusively in Camden Superstores. All three of my brothers have sunk money in the brewery. And Gertie has postponed charging me rent on the barn—or charging me for her advice and tasting expertise—as her investment."

"Wow. That's a lot of people depending on you to succeed," Lexie observed, feeling a twinge of guilt for taking him away from his work last night just to show her around the damage in the little house.

Micah merely inclined his head in acknowledgment as he tasted his bratwurst.

Then his eyebrows rose when that flavor registered. After swallowing his bite, he said, "But that's pretty good… What do you think?"

Lexie let her own eyebrows arch as she finished chewing and swallowing, too.

"I agree—that's *good*," she said emphatically. "There's an earthy, spicy, just-the-right-amount-of-bitter-with-a-little-tang-to-it taste. Is that from the beer?"

Micah laughed. "You have Gertie's sensitive taste buds?"

Lexie shrugged. "I don't know. Do I?"

"To pick out that much of what I'm going for in my hops and in my stout blend, even when it's mixed in as just one of the flavors in the bratwurst? I'd say so."

"Are your hops different than other hops?"

"I spent five years crossbreeding them until I came up with exactly what I wanted. They're my own hybrid. They're *my* secret."

"You did that *while* you were in the Marines?"

"Yeah. Experimenting with the hops and with

the brewing were a sideline. Something I did whenever I was stationary."

"I didn't know you were interested in botany."

"I was *interested* in making beer. The botany part just came from being the grandson of a farmer."

"In high school, you were into chemistry," she recalled. "We teased you about becoming a mad scientist. And I know you always liked to *drink* beer—when we could get our hands on it. Did those two things mix when you started hanging out with my grandmother?" It was another guess because brewing beer was not something he'd ever mentioned when they'd been friends.

"It did."

So this was an interest that had sparked after the barn incident.

He stood up from the picnic bench and took his plate with him. "I'm having a second brat—I think they're great. Want another one?"

"One is my limit. But they *are* great," she agreed. "I have a chocolate cupcake recipe that calls for stout in it—after tasting it in these, I think it might be good in those, too. If the stout is too bitter, it ruins them but yours isn't."

"You put beer in chocolate cupcakes?" he said, sounding doubtful about the combination.

"I spent a year working with a pastry chef in New Orleans. He was a horrible ogre but I came

away with pretty much the same skills he had—
or else my head would have rolled."

"So baker is one of the skills in your jack-of-
all-trades arsenal?"

"It is."

"Why did you stay working with an ogre for a
whole year?"

"I liked the job, just not the boss. Of course, that
could be said of a lot of jobs I had. Or the reverse."

"But you like to bake and you know how to run
a bakery?"

"I do," she confirmed, not sure why he seemed
to find it important.

"Are you good at it?" he persisted.

"I've been told I am. The ogre was furious when
I quit—he thought I was leaving to open my own
shop to compete with him. When I said we were
moving away, he softened up a little and said I'd
been his best apprentice."

"Hmm…" Micah mused as he ate a few chips.

Lexie had one of those, too, giving him a curious look even as she drank in the sight of that
sculpted face of his.

When he'd finished his chips, he said, "In that
case, I heard something today that you might be
interested in."

"What did you hear?" she played along.

"Nessa Bryant has decided to retire. She's selling the bakery in town. Maybe you should think about taking it over."

Lexie laughed at that notion. "I sent Gram a little money out of my paychecks now and then over the years—without Jason knowing—so we'd have a nest egg when we came back. It's all mine now but there isn't enough to *buy* a bakery."

"One of the things I've learned with the brewery is that you have to put some creative thinking into how to bankroll yourself. What if Nessa agreed to carry the loan? You could offer her a down payment and set up a payment plan with her—it would be like a retirement supplement that could give her income every month while you paid it off," he suggested, sounding very businesslike. And very unlike the boy she used to know.

"Or who knows," he went on, "the bank might take a risk on a business loan for you—you're a hometown girl, your family helped found Merritt way back when. Factor in that the bakery is a staple around here, a meeting place on top of supplying breads and rolls and goodies for everything that goes on, and that's more incentive to give you the backing to keep it going. Can you make wedding cakes?"

"I can and I have. I made Jill's…" And was this possibility really starting to gel?

"So here's an idea," Micah said as something

seemed to occur to him. "There's a food festival coming up—"

"I saw the signs on my way through town to Jill's."

"I'm renting a booth. It'll be the first public outing for my beers—well, not for the flavored stouts, they're not perfected yet and I need Gertie for that. But what if you make your beer cupcakes, sell them at the booth, too, and see how they go over?"

"Using your plain stout?"

"Cupcakes and beer," he said with a laugh. "It'll give the booth some novelty if nothing else."

Was that his motive?

It was just so difficult for Lexie not to be suspicious of Micah. Tonight—like last night—felt again like old times. Old times talking, supporting each other, problem solving together... But could she trust that?

"Let me think about it," she hedged.

"I have three different stouts—want to taste the one that's in the brats straight from the bottle and the other two, too? Then you can choose which one might work the best in your cupcakes—*if* you decide to make them? We can do a tasting right now."

They'd both cleaned their plates and were done eating. So were they going to just sit here and drink beer together?

That didn't seem wise.

But it *was* a good idea for her to taste all the options and choose…

"Okay," she said.

He again stood up from the picnic table, went into the house and returned with three bottles of beer that she'd seen in the fridge but not thought much about.

"We bottled these last week," he said as he opened each one and gave her samples of them all in the paper cups he'd also brought out.

She tried them, one by one. "Ooh, I think the second one would be even better in my cupcakes than the one that was in the brats. It's richer—I think it will bulk up the chocolate."

"I think you really do have Gertie's taste buds," he responded. "And her oven didn't get damaged so you could use it…"

"I'm still thinking about it," she insisted.

He offered her more beer. She refilled her small cup with the one she'd chosen as the best for her cupcakes and he took the third blend for himself, drinking it from the bottle.

"That was always your response," he said as they settled into enjoying his libations. *"Let me think about it,"* he mimicked her playfully. "You weighed the pros and cons, made your lists."

"And you were our daredevil," she countered, realizing only after she'd said it that it had come out fondly, unclouded by resentment.

But it felt kind of nice so she ran with it. "You were always determined to test every limit—"

"We had some fun," he reminded. "How about when the four of us sledded down Dead Man's Hill on that old door?"

"Oh, that *was* fun," she confirmed.

"And kayaking down the river when it was close to flooding?"

"Dangerous but also fun," she decreed. "Not to mention a lot of trouble afterward when we got caught sneaking the kayak we'd *borrowed* back…"

"Worth it," he judged.

"And there was our horse rescue…" she said.

"Hey, I was going to do that alone," he pointed out. "You guys wanted in."

"Because those sleazy people who had moved in outside of town had trapped that wild stallion and were abusing it."

"So we set it free," Micah concluded.

Another good—and heroic—deed that he was responsible for. Like the things Jill had told her about today.

Was it just that one incident with her where he'd gone wrong?

"Since I was only a kid, I didn't think the sheriff would believe me if I told him what I'd seen," Micah reminisced. "Seemed like the logical thing to do was just let the horse loose. Those creeps didn't have any right to him anyway—it wasn't like they'd paid for him."

"But four fourteen-year-olds skulking around private property at two in the morning? Not smart. *We* could have ended up their next captives and no one would have known where we were." She shivered with the memory. "I was glad when those people left town."

Micah seconded that by raising his beer to her and she instantly became much too aware of his big strong hand around the bottle.

When he took a swig then, she drank from her own cup, needing the beer to wash back whatever it was that had reared up in her in response to him.

But instead another memory cropped up. It made her laugh even before she said, "What about the night you talked us into climbing that tree to watch the seventh-grade history teacher and the school nurse parked up at Potter's Point?"

He grimaced. "Yeah, in hindsight all four of us on one branch was bad planning—I should have known the branch would break and dump us onto the hood of Mr. Snyder's car."

"And before we got to see anything but kissing even though you were sure they were *doing it*."

"But that was some steamy kissing," he defended with a devilish laugh.

It had been.

And why remembering it caused her to wonder about Micah's kissing skills, Lexie didn't know.

What's going on with you? she demanded of herself.

Hearing Gertie's and Jill's praise of Micah, combined with remembering some past good deeds, seemed to have opened up a soft spot in her.

She couldn't let that get too far, though. Especially not when her thoughts verged on sensual.

She sat up straighter, glanced around at the darkening sky, then at the remnants of their dinner on the table and said, "Since you cooked, if you need to go back to work, I can clean this up."

Her tone was aloof now, and she saw the way it made those full eyebrows of his pulse together in confusion.

What she didn't know was why she regretted it once she'd done it. Why she was sorry to conclude their evening together.

"You're sure?" he said, sounding tentative.

"I'm sure," she said too firmly.

He nodded, and she thought she glimpsed sad acceptance in it. Then he placed both big hands flat on the picnic table and pushed himself to his feet.

"Okay." He hoisted one leg over the bench seat and then the other. "How 'bout we bring dinner over to Gertie and Mary tomorrow night?" he suggested then.

"I'm sure they'd like that," Lexie said, knowing her grandmother would be thrilled and recognizing that the gesture was thoughtful of him. "I'll tell them when I go over in the morning. I'm babysitting for Jill in the afternoon while she goes to the dentist and then I'll be home."

"Gertie loves the burritos from a Mexican food place that's in town now. If that sounds good to her, we can bring those."

It was something Lexie didn't know about her grandmother that *he* did.

Something that said another good thing about him.

But she pushed that thought out of her head along with everything else that was confusing her tonight.

"I'll talk to her about it," she said, looking at his handsome face and trying not to appreciate just how striking it was.

"See you tomorrow, then," he said.

"See you tomorrow," Lexie echoed, beginning to gather the things on the table.

There was still plenty of beer in the bottle she'd been pouring from or she might have been able to blame the liquor for the fact that as Micah headed across the yard to the barn she couldn't keep from watching him.

Long thick legs. Glorious derriere. Narrow

waist. Broad powerful shoulders stretching his T-shirt as far as it would go…

Once upon a time, she'd liked him…

She didn't know where that thought had come from but there it was.

But yes, she *had* liked him, even if it had been only as a friend.

What if those fond feelings were cropping up again?

That might be risky, she warned herself as she forced her eyes away from his backside.

Risky and unwise after the lesson she'd learned.

And it seemed even less wise when, all on its own, her head raised so she could get one last glimpse of Micah.

Oh, definitely risky and unwise, she thought when she realized that just around the edges of those fonder feelings was a hint of something else.

Something that seemed like…

Attraction?

No…

That couldn't be…

She'd never been attracted to him before.

She certainly couldn't be now, post-barn-incident. And yet *something* was going on with her that she didn't understand. That she didn't *want* going on with her.

She might have agreed to be pleasant, she might have recalled—thanks to Jill and to their conversation tonight—that there had been good days with Micah along with the bad, but when it came to her thoughts about him?

Uh-uh.

She just wasn't going to let herself forget what he'd done.

Chapter Five

"You look like hell, boy. And what are you doin' here? First Tanner shows up at four thirty and now you at barely 6:00 a.m.? You boys have something going that takes two of you to tell me?"

"Tanner's here?" Micah asked his grandfather in surprise when he got out of his truck at the family home Tuesday morning.

It was common for Ben to have his first cup of coffee sitting in one of the white rocking chairs on the front porch. That was where he was when Micah drove up. Nothing unusual about that.

But the mention of Micah's brother Tanner?

"What are you talking about?" Micah asked. "Tanner is deployed overseas."

The elderly man shook his head, then nodded in the direction of the front door. "Four thirty this morning," he repeated. "The damn fool's lucky I didn't shoot him. Heard the porch creak and came downstairs with my shotgun."

"You didn't know he was coming?"

"Not a clue."

"Is he all right?"

"Says he is. Said it was a last-minute thing. But something's up."

"He isn't saying what he's doing here?"

Ben shrugged. "Says he has something he has to check out. Didn't look happy about it, whatever it is. Kind of like you—you look like you've been ridden hard and put away wet. What's up?"

"No crisis, I just pulled an all-nighter and haven't been to bed yet. I was in the brewery ruining fifteen gallons of stout." Not ideal, but hardly an emergency.

Tanner, on the other hand... Nothing short of a family emergency would be reason enough for him to get leave and a transport back to the States from a deployment.

But as far as Micah knew, there weren't any emergencies—family or otherwise. He'd spoken to both of the other triplets, Quinn and Dalton, yesterday and they were fine. Ben was sitting right there, also fine. Micah was fine, and that was their whole family. Well, except for the extended part of the Camdens, but Micah had also talked to their cousin Beau last night and there were no emergencies on that front, either.

His grandfather seemed less curious about it and more focused on Micah's early-morning visit. "When I called last night to tell you that picture frame was ready, I didn't mean for you to rush over at the crack of dawn."

"I know. I just want to get it back to Lexie."

"I could have brought it over. Especially if you're so busy you're workin' through the night. Things goin' bad with the beer?"

"No, not bad," Micah was quick to reassure him. "I'm just still working to get the flavored stouts right. Last night I guess maybe I overdid the add-ins? I'm not quite sure. But whatever I did wrong, I ended up with swill. The plain stouts are all still solid, though—in fact, Lexie and I both loved your bratwurst. You have a big hit with that one."

"I thought so, too. Want to make sausage-flavored beer?" Ben joked.

"Uh… I'll pass on that."

"Anything else I can do at the brewery to help out?"

"Nah, thanks. It's all trial and error. Eventually I'll get it right. I'm seeing Gertie tonight—I'll run a few things by her, see what she thinks, and that'll help."

"How is she?"

Micah told him what he knew.

Then Ben said, "Well, you still look like hell. Tanner's sleepin' up in his room   why don't you shower and catch a few hours in yours?"

A lack of sleep definitely wasn't helping anything. He'd left instructions for his staff on how to start the day so he knew they could—and would—go to work without him. And if he went back to the Parker place to rest, he'd have to stretch out in the sunroom—which was great when it was dark, not so great for sleeping after sunup. And a few hours nap in his own bed sounded pretty good right then.

"I might do that," he said.

"Go for it. I'm headed into town after a while. If I'm not here when you get up, there's food in the fridge. The frame is waiting for you on the entry table."

"Thanks for doing that for me."

"Just get some rest. And shower—you smell like a brewery," Ben said, amused by his own quip.

Micah reached down and squeezed his grandfather's bony shoulder as he went past him into the house. He trudged up the stairs to his room.

His grandfather was right—he *did* smell like a brewery, he realized as he stripped off his clothes to get in the shower in the connecting bathroom. He was so used to the smell—so overexposed to it from the endless hours of work—that he barely noticed it unless someone pointed it out.

The brewery that he had so much riding on and so many people pulling for. So many people who he didn't want to—and couldn't—disappoint.

But the previous night's fiascos were eating at him.

Failure was just not an option. Not even if it meant he had to lose some sleep, he thought as he stepped under the spray of water.

But he'd really thought he was closer to success with those flavored stouts. He'd thought the last batches were going to work.

And they'd ended up the worst yet.

He scrubbed hard and then washed his hair, too, fighting a heavy wave of discouragement.

Don't go there, he cautioned himself as he stood under the water to rinse the lather. *Take your lumps and keep at it...*

But damn if there hadn't been a lot of lumps to take...

The beer failures.

The tree damage.

The disaster with Adrianna...

He could make a solid argument for the disaster with Adrianna not being his fault but he refused to let himself off the hook. It *was* his fault that what Adrianna had seen from him—and heard from his mother—had led her to her decision.

And the mess with Adrianna was the toughest lump to take. The costliest. The one with the outcome that he couldn't fix…

Wow, he was carrying some heavy stuff with him today, he realized.

Lack of sleep, that's all it is, he told himself as he turned off the water.

But once he dried off and got into bed, hands behind his head on the pillow, sleep didn't come instantly the way he'd expected it to. The way he needed it to.

Instead, his mind kept chewing on that argument with Adrianna, especially the part where she'd used lack of sleep as her justification.

So what if a baby would have kept him up at night when he was home? He would have found a way to make it work. He would have found a way to make it *all* work.

Just like now, when he would find a way to fix Gertie's and Lexie's houses despite his other problems.

Not that Lexie believed him any more than Adrianna had…

Lexie…

Well, hey, it had been maybe fifteen or twenty minutes without thinking about her.

He should probably count that as a victory…

He sighed, pressing deeper into the pillow, hoping to drift off.

But still he was restless. Exhausted and restless. It was starting again.

Thinking about Lexie almost every minute.

Noticing her hair, her eyes, her nose, her lips, her body...

Loving it when he made her laugh.

Wanting to be with her so much that he'd taken time he shouldn't have taken away from the brewery.

Looking over at the back of her grandmother's house a million times a day, hoping to catch a glimpse of her.

It was puberty all over again...

Not that he had a crush on her like he'd had then. He didn't. Of course not.

But he had this awareness of her that he just couldn't seem to shake. No matter how hard he tried to fight it, she was just there, in his mind. Day and night.

And it didn't help that things seemed to be getting better between them. For the past two nights, there had been moments almost like when they were friends. He'd always liked talking to her and it seemed like they might have found their way back to that.

He did want things between them to be amicable, he reminded himself. He didn't want animosity to tinge his relationship with her grandmother.

But it was going beyond amicable to crave the

scent of her when she first came downstairs after a shower. To long for the chance to run his hands through her hair. To want to bury his face in the side of her neck…

None of that had anything to do with Gertie.

Just keep the mission in mind, he told himself, trying to call upon his military training.

The primary mission was to make beer. To make the brewery succeed.

The secondary mission was to repair those houses.

The Marines had taught him focus and he needed to draw on that discipline now.

Lexie wasn't the enemy but there was bad blood between them and he definitely needed to resist this draw toward her.

He already had more than a full plate.

And if those weren't grounds enough, there was also the fact that she hadn't ever seen him as more than a friend. How dumb would he have to be to let himself fall for her again when his feelings would never be returned?

Pretty dumb, he concluded.

So block it!

That's what he was going to do, he resolved with conviction.

But as he finally began to drift off, the image of Lexie's face kept him company.

And so did that quiet urge to do whatever he could to be with her…

* * *

When Lexie went downstairs Tuesday morning, she found a note from Micah telling her that a vet work crew was coming the next day to frame the side wall of the bigger house. Then they were going to camp overnight in the backyard and frame the side of the little house on Thursday.

In response to that news, when she returned from visiting Gertie, she spent the day preparing her grandmother's house for construction—moving things out of the way, placing protective tarps over what needed to stay in place, and taping up clear plastic dividers to keep construction dust and debris out of the undamaged sections.

She planned to do the same in the little house the next day while the construction crew worked on her grandmother's house. Then she used the rest of Tuesday afternoon baking two large pans of brownies. She cut a few to bring to her grandmother and Mary—the rest she put away for the coming construction crew.

Just before five o'clock, she showered and changed into a clean pair of her new jeans and a previously unworn red top with small frills that formed cap sleeves—it was what Lily had called a casual date outfit. Not that she and Micah taking dinner to her grandmother and cousin was a date. Instead, she told herself that the red blouse was bright and cheery—the perfect outfit for visiting someone who was ailing.

She applied her makeup—adding a touch more eyeliner than usual, plus mascara and a hint of shadow—and left her hair loose around her shoulders.

Lastly came a pair of ballet shoes before she went downstairs and found Micah waiting for her.

He again had on a military-issue T-shirt—this one white and tight enough to make any normal, healthy woman's mouth water. He also wore a pair of jeans that highlighted thick thighs, a narrow waist and a derriere to die for.

His face was still stubbled but the short scruff was trimmed and neat, and he smelled freshly showered and unfairly wonderful.

But recalling her resolve of the night before not to lose sight of his treachery from the past, she worked to not let it affect her.

Micah drove and after a stop in town to pick up Gertie's new favorite Mexican food, they went to Mary's apartment.

It was an evening of burritos, green chili, a delicate rice flecked with red peppers, guacamole, chips and jovial conversation during which Lexie told her grandmother about Micah's idea that she consider buying the bakery.

Gertie was enthusiastically in favor of it and as

she took her third brownie, Mary chimed in with her support, too.

What Lexie found the most interesting through the evening, though, was what she witnessed between Gertie and Micah.

They really had become the best of buddies and an impressive team when it came to talking about their favorite subject—brewing beer.

Until witnessing it, Lexie hadn't realized just how much of a bond had formed between them. How much of a genuine connection they'd made. And she found herself having the oddest reaction to it.

It made her a little jealous.

Although she couldn't tell whether she was jealous that Micah seemed to feel every bit as close to Gertie as she was herself, or if she was jealous of what her grandmother shared with Micah...

"I don't know what I'd do without your Gram," he said as they got into his truck to return home.

"You two really love that whole beer-making thing..." Lexie responded.

"Sorry, did I monopolize Gertie?"

Anxious to cover up any hint of jealousy—no matter what was causing it—Lexie said, "No, I talked to her about the bakery idea. And she was in her glory talking beer with you—I wouldn't have taken that away from her."

Then she changed the subject. "I heard Gram

say that she thinks you need to add your flavorings in stages?" she said. "Add some when the wort is cooling, more later and then more at the cold crash—whatever wort and cold crashing are?"

"Wort is the liquid that comes out of mixing the malt grains and hops with hot water—that's the start of the process. Cold crashing is when we cool the stout to near-freezing temps, just before bottling it—the end of the line. Gertie thinks I should hold off on a fuller fruit infusion until the end, when the beer is cold and the yeast is dormant so the sugars in the fruits won't ferment. I think that was what I did wrong with my last batch." The excitement that had come to life in him while he and Gertie hashed through his problems was clear in his voice.

Lexie ran with it. "I had another thought—well, three, actually—when you guys were talking about flavorings," she said tentatively.

"Let's hear 'em."

"I was just thinking about adding flavors to things I bake. If I bake anything lemon or orange, I always add fresh peel into the batter and use it as a garnish, too. I wondered if putting a curl of orange and lemon peel in each bottle at the end might brighten your citrus stout and give you a last hint of sweet-tart flavor."

"I could try that," he allowed.

"For your sour cherry stout, I was thinking that

whenever I bake cherry-anything, I put in a touch of almond—you don't necessarily taste it but it boosts the cherry flavor. I wondered if the same might be true in beer."

"Hmm… Okay. I'll test it out. And number three?"

"I worked in a bakery in New Mexico for a stretch, too. They made a lot of breads with peppers in them. I heard you tell Gram that you're using habaneros but you don't think they're giving you enough flavor, so I was thinking you might want to mix in either roasted New Mexico green chilies or chipotles. The chilies would give you an earthier taste while the chipotles would add a smoky flavor."

He took his eyes off the road to glance at her. "Okay…" he said again, this time as if he were impressed. "Those are all good ideas. That's the sort of thing Gertie helps with but she mainly thinks in terms of the beer. Coming at it from a baker's perspective is a new twist."

He looked ahead again and then said, "So what did you think about Gertie's idea that you be my taster while she's on meds for her leg?"

What Lexie had thought was that her grandmother was trying to push them into spending more time together.

But when that hint of jealousy gave her another little jab and made her think of the warmth between her grandmother and Micah over their common interest, she found herself saying, "I'm not a beer expert, but I guess I could tell you when I think something tastes good or bad, when there's enough or too much of the other flavors."

"She said to taste at each stage," he reminded.

"So you're just going to keep me drunk?" Lexie joked.

He laughed. "Now there's a thought… But, no, you just need a swig to tell if I'm on the right track. You won't be drinking anywhere near enough to get drunk."

"I suppose I can do that," she agreed before she heard herself say out of nowhere, "It's kind of strange to see the way you and Gram are now."

"How so?"

She shrugged. "I know you were always close, but years ago it was more of an adult-child sort of thing—I mean, even though you were seventeen, you weren't really an adult so it wasn't like two equals. Two friends. But now—"

"Yeah, I guess it just evolved. I've seen her every time I've come home over the years. We wrote, emailed—beer was the main topic but she always asked what I was doing and kept tabs on me. I did the same with her. I guess along the way I grew up and yeah, we became friends."

"Friends with the same obsession," Lexie qualified. Maybe that was what made them seem so close. Anyone seeing the two of them together would think that Gertie was his grandmother, that he was her grandson.

"We *are* both obsessed with beer," he conceded.

"She always liked making her home brews—it was her hobby. But now it seems like it's given her a new lease on life." It was no wonder Gertie had let him put his brewery in her backyard so she could be an active part of it. But Lexie wasn't convinced that was what was best for her grandmother.

"You say that like it might be bad. Isn't a new lease on life a good thing?" Micah asked, apparently hearing the uncertainty in her voice.

"Sure, but…"

But it *did* concern Lexie that he might let Gertie down. "I just wouldn't want you to learn what you need to learn from her and then…you know, cast her aside or something…"

"Cast her aside?" he repeated. "Like I'm just using her?"

"I hope not," Lexie said.

Micah shot her another glance. "You have no idea how much your grandmother means to me," he said seriously. "Or how much I owe her."

"Because she taught you about beer?" Lexie said with some skepticism.

"It's more than that. A lot more. She stuck by me when she probably shouldn't have. And she was a better influence on me than my own mother was."

"Your mother was a bad influence on you?"

"In a lot of ways. Not that she was a bad mother," he added. "She just had some screwy ideas."

"Like what?"

"You know that my great-grandfather—Hector— was H.J. Camden's brother—"

"And H.J. Camden was the guy who made a gazillion dollars with Camden Superstores."

"Actually H.J. made a gazillion dollars even before there were superstores—he was the guy who built the whole empire *behind* the superstores. The two brothers—Hector and H.J.—started in the same place. They grew up in Northbridge on the family's farm that they inherited together. But while my great-grandfather was content as a simple farmer, H.J. had much bigger plans."

"Superstores?"

"That idea was actually Hector's," Micah said. "But that came later. At first, back on the farm, H.J. started his wheeling and dealing, buying up anything he could just to *own* as much as he could—"

"Whether it was on the up and up or not—isn't that what they say about him?"

"It is. But, anyway, my great-grandfather just wasn't as ambitious as H.J. was and he didn't like being around all the wheeling and dealing. Hector wanted a simple farm life. So he sold his half of the Northbridge place to H.J. and came to Merritt. But once H.J. had accumulated land and lumber mills and mines and factories and what have you, it was Hector's idea that H.J. open a general store—because general stores sell pretty much everything and H.J. had his fingers in so many different industries. One big general store would be a place for H.J. to sell all he was producing from his other holdings without a middleman cutting into his profits."

"So the superstores were your great-grandfather's idea? Doesn't that mean he should have had a cut or something?"

"Now you're thinking like my mom. That rubbed her wrong—even though Hector always said that H.J. offered him a partnership in the first store but that he turned it down. He still didn't want the pressure of H.J.'s ambitions."

"Or maybe he didn't want any part of H.J.'s dirty dealings?"

"Could be," Micah admitted with a shrug. "All I know is that no matter what else went on, Hector and H.J. were always close."

"Just not close enough for your family to end up with a share of the wealth—"

"The way my mom thought we should have," Micah finished for her. "It ate at her even before my dad was killed flying the Camden private plane—which poured fuel onto the flames."

"I knew your dad was a pilot in the air force— I thought that was how he died."

Micah shook his head. "He served in the air force, which is why my brothers and I were all sort of drawn to the military—following in his footsteps. But when Dad got out of the air force, he went to work piloting a private plane for H.J. and his family. We lived in Denver then, until I was three and Dad was killed in the plane crash along with H.J.'s son and both of his grandsons and their wives."

"But not H.J.?"

"H.J. was home laid up with a bad back, being taken care of by his daughter-in-law—we've always called her GiGi. She and H.J. ended up raising my ten Camden cousins who were orphaned by the crash."

"We've known each other since we were kids but I never knew all this," Lexie marveled.

"Family history—it's not like it's sandbox chit-chat."

Lexie conceded to that. But she returned to what he'd been saying about his father. "So your dad was flying the plane?"

"It wasn't pilot error. It was mechanical," Micah was quick to add. "That was the second thing that my Mom resented, the biggest thing was that she lost her husband because he was *working for* that rich side of the family. She held on to those two grudges the rest of her life. It made her kind of an angry, resentful, intense person."

"And that made her a bad influence on you?"

"Partly. Plus, somewhere in her head, as much as she blamed the other Camdens, she also blamed Hector and my grandfather and my dad," Micah explained. "Don't get me wrong—she loved them all, she was devoted to them. But she also fixated on the idea that if they'd been more ambitious, more aggressive—the way H.J. and his son and grandsons had been—then we would have had a share in the superstores and that would have changed everything. Maybe then my grandfather wouldn't have settled for just running a small family farm, and maybe my dad would have been something more than the hired hand of the rich Camdens."

They'd arrived home by then, but Lexie still didn't understand how his mother's perspective had made Gertie a better influence on him than his mother. And she honestly wanted to know.

So rather than saying good-night and going upstairs, she went with him into the kitchen and prompted him to go on by saying, "Okay, your mom had some baggage…"

Micah leaned his hip against the edge of the countertop and crossed his arms over his very flat stomach, extending his legs and crossing them at the ankles, too.

"That *baggage*," he went on, "translated into some strong ideas about the kind of men her sons needed to be."

"She didn't just want you to be good men?" Lexie said as she found a spot against the edge of the kitchen table, facing him.

"My mother wanted us to go after whatever we wanted with a vengeance. H.J.'s kind of vengeance. She was hell-bent on raising us to be men who were as hard-hitting and ambitious and undefeatable as the other side of the family had been."

"But the rumors were that they were ruthless, too."

"I don't ever remember her using that word..." he hedged. "But she did foster really extreme competitiveness. Anything we wanted, the question was always, *How bad do you want it?* If it was the last cookie, getting our driver's licenses, borrowing the car, you name it—that's what she said. Followed by, *Show me how bad you want it...* Usually, convincing her meant we had to do more chores, give up allowance, bite the bullet on something she knew we didn't want to do—whatever it took to let her see that we were willing to go to all lengths to overcome any obstacle."

"Didn't that just lead to kids who never took no for an answer?"

He chuckled at that. "Sometimes we *did* take no for an answer just because it was easier—but then she made it clear how disappointed she was, how worried it made her that we would settle. She'd lecture us about how no one who settled got anywhere in life. She'd praise whoever showed initiative and determination, and…I guess you could say she'd shame whoever didn't. So yeah, kids who took no for an answer were *not* what she wanted."

"And when it was something that more than one of you were competing for, didn't that cause a lot of fights?"

"With four boys? Oh, yeah," he confirmed with another laugh. "There were a *lot* of fights. And undercutting and backstabbing and wrangling and outmaneuvering and ratting each other out and—"

"Nothing came without that?"

"Christmas and birthday gifts were freebies. But other than those? Every privilege, every decision about where to go, what to eat, how the work around the farm was doled out, any extra money we asked for, a cool pair of boots or an unnecessary new jacket or shirt—"

"I had no idea that's how she brought you up," Lexie said. This cast new light on how competitive he'd been with Jason, how much more strong-willed he'd been all the way around than the rest of them. It seemed like such a strange—and subtly harsh—way of growing up. "What about your grandfather? Did he do that, too?"

"No. He softened the message some—it was Pops who would talk about us being good men. His expectations and example probably kept us all from going too far—most of the time, anyway."

Micah paused, gave her a regret-filled frown and said, "Not when it came to the barn thing, but other times…"

Another moment's silence followed that before he went on.

"But Big Ben was careful to stay on the sidelines—there was no question that we were raised by our mother. He never once crossed or contradicted her. Even if we went to him with a complaint about her, he supported her and refused to even mediate. *Your mom is the boss*—that's what he'd always say."

"So that's it—it was her way all the way, even if her way was sort of extreme?"

"Mom thought she was helping us, toughening us up so we'd be like H.J. So we'd be successful."

"It just sounds so severe," Lexie ventured.

"Maybe…" was as far as he would go to agree with that. "But I do know that it made us all good candidates for the military—although Mom was hoping more for business moguls or titans of industry," Micah said. "But I think it was lucky that we all did go military—the military took the drive and discipline she'd cultivated and put a better spin on it. That's where we learned the kind of brotherhood that Pops had tried to encourage in us—"

"He didn't succeed?"

"His message that we were family, that we should stand up for each other, worked when it was one of us against an outsider—none of us were going to let the others get pushed around. But at home it just couldn't survive the mentality that Mom wanted us to have—we were fierce competitors there."

"Because you were pitted against each other to get what you wanted," Lexie noted. "It seems sad to me that you all had to join the service to learn to be brothers."

Micah shrugged that off. "The important thing is that we *did* learn it. Before that, we were kids and kids don't have the best judgment. Not using my determination productively was how I got into trouble that last year of high school—not only with you but with the law, too," he said. "I wanted to brew beer, so I brewed beer. I wanted to make money from it, so I sold it—even though I knew it was illegal as a minor to make and sell alcohol, especially to other minors."

"Which got you arrested," Lexie filled in. She'd heard about it through the grapevine at the time, despite all her efforts to avoid it.

"Which got me arrested," he confirmed. "But

not until after the sheriff had given me one warning, and then brought me in front of a judge for a lecture and a fine that took a chunk of my proceeds. When those two reprimands weren't strong enough noes for me, he finally arrested me. I was arraigned in juvenile court and given the choice—either the judge was going to try me as an adult because I was a week from turning eighteen, or I could go into the military…" He paused and said in an aside, "Gertie never knew about the warning or the fine."

"She won't hear it from me. But if you think she hasn't heard about it somewhere along the line, I think you're being naive."

"Probably," he said with another chuckle.

Only now Lexie was even more confused. "I hate to point this out, but it was my grandmother who taught you about brewing beer… Doesn't that make her as bad of an influence on you as your mother was?"

"No," he said, giving her a look as if she were missing something. "What Gertie taught me gave me a skill and a goal. What I turned around and did with it was all on me. Gertie was nothing but a good influence."

"Because she was loving and caring and—"

His laughter at that cut her words short.

"Sorry," he said when he stopped laughing. "I'll grant you that my mother's how-bad-do-you-want-it stuff was a little warped but other than that she was very loving and caring. That wasn't what I lacked. Gertie helped by being hard as nails on me."

"It didn't seem that way," Lexie refuted.

"Because you weren't there listening to her!"

The thought that Gertie might have been harder on him than Lexie had known gave her a little satisfaction. "So she wasn't just taking you under her wing and excusing what you'd done to me."

"Oh, hell no! Gertie read me the riot act over it and lectured me until she was blue in the face. She made no bones about the fact that I was a rotten friend to you and Jason both—which had never occurred to me," he confessed wryly.

"You kept coming around…" Lexie reminded.

"The lecturing didn't go on forever or I probably wouldn't have."

"She didn't dwell on it because she knew how your mom was and couldn't hold you completely responsible?"

"No, she didn't know what went on in my house."

"Then she just forgave you," Lexie tried again, attempting to understand her grandmother's motivation.

Micah was looking very intently at her and she had the sense that he thought she was playing some kind of game with him. But his expression lost all humor and after a moment he said, "Gertie cut me some slack because she understood why I'd done what I did with you."

"If she didn't know what went on in your house, how could she understand you pouncing on someone else's misfortune for your own benefit?"

"And again you're thinking that my own *benefit* was what? Looking like a big man or a stud?"

"Yes," Lexie said, standing her ground. "Or to stick it to Jason," she added.

He shook his head. "I told you, boosting my reputation at your expense was *not* what I wanted. And Gertie understood that."

"What did she understand? What *did* you want?" Lexie demanded.

"Come on, Lexie, you had to have known."

"I had to have known what?" she challenged. "That you were competitive? Sure, I knew that. I knew that you used me to needle Jason about being *soft* because he was with me, that you thought you were more of a man because you didn't let yourself get *stuck* with one girl. I knew that you always had to prove you were better than Jason at every sport, every game. What else am I supposed to know?"

"I did feel competitive with Jason—you're right about that," he acknowledged. "But I was competing with him because of how I felt about you…"

His deep voice had grown even deeper and so quiet it was barely audible.

"How you *felt* about me? What does that mean?

We were friends, and then you turned on me—what changed? Did I do something that aggravated you? Did you feel like I'd taken Jason away from you? Is that why you always called Jill by her first name but started calling me *Parker*—like we were barely friends anymore? Is that why you gave me such a hard time about everything? Why you made fun of Jason and me being together? Why you told him all the time that he was dumb to let himself be tied down with me?"

"It was all just a cover," Micah said, putting the brakes on her outpouring. "A cover for what Gertie had seen in me. For what she'd guessed was going on with me—"

"*What* was going on with you?" Lexie nearly shouted.

Micah hesitated, then spoke. "What Gertie knew and the reason she had mercy on me was that I liked you…"

Lexie could only stare in shock and disbelief.

"It's true. I liked you. Too much. I had for years—since we'd started middle school, about the same time Jason went after you. I did, too—I tried to impress you, to win you over, to make you see me as more than a friend, but he was better at it than I was." Micah shook his head as if at his own ineptness.

"But after that day in the barn," he went on, "when the rumors started flying, I thought I saw my chance. I thought if Jason believed we'd gotten together in the barn that he'd break up with you. And then maybe I could have you. So I took the opportunity. Because you were what I wanted and I went after you in any way I could think of."

Plain and simple.

She had honestly never considered this possibility and it wasn't easy now to adjust that thinking.

As if he knew the message needed reinforcing, he said, "The bottom line was that I had the biggest crush on you."

Was *that* what Gertie had been talking about seeing in him? Not his overly competitiveness with Jason?

It must have been…

"I fought it," Micah was saying. "I tried everything to squelch it. I tried going after other girls. I tried to ignore it. I wished it away. But whenever I saw you…" He sighed helplessly. "Then that day at the barn happened and the gossip started and I still wanted you so much I could taste it. I thought it was my opening. So no matter how ill-conceived it was, I went for it the way I was supposed to go for anything I wanted—full steam ahead…"

Wreaking havoc on her life in the process. Permanently hurting her relationship with her father.

In light of the consequences, how could she feel anything but anger and resentment for him?

But she did. She was starting to feel glimmers

of sympathy, of compassion, of understanding for the young Micah. The kind of sympathy and compassion and understanding her grandmother must have felt for him.

That made so much more sense...

"It was a stupid, desperate kid move," Micah was saying. "And Gertie recognized that. So after raking me over the coals for it, and making sure I was well aware of what a rotten thing it had been to do to you and Jason, she took pity on me." Micah paused and after another moment said, "And since then I've been so damn sorry..."

It was the explanation and apology he'd been trying to give since she'd returned to Merritt.

An apology that was genuine. Heartfelt. Raw and full of tangible remorse and regret.

She couldn't seem to stop it from deflating some of her righteous indignation.

Then he seemed to draw himself up out of the past, pull himself together and said, "Gertie's lectures, the things she made me see—coming on top of what my grandfather had tried to teach along the way—finally made me start to reevaluate what my mother had drummed into me and my brothers. The Marine Corps took care of the rest, teaching me how important it is to be loyal, to have loyalty from other people, to act honorably. That's when my mindset finally got channeled in a better direction. But if it hadn't been for Gertie," he said, "I might have ended up in jail instead."

Lexie didn't know what to say, torn between new sympathy and long-held pain.

Silence fell for a few moments.

Then Micah said, "So one more time—*I am sorry.*"

Lexie nodded, knowing—believing now—that that was true but still not quite able to grant forgiveness.

"And don't ever think," he continued, "that I will *cast your grandmother aside.* She's as much family to me as she is to you. Without her, I wouldn't be who I am—which, believe it or not, is very different from who you used to know."

Lexie still needed more evidence before she could truly accept that.

But for the first time, she could concede that he might actually have changed into the better man her grandmother contended that he was.

And what she knew now did alleviate her fear that he might let down her grandmother in some way—so that was good...

Lexie had the impression that he'd said all he was going to say. That seemed confirmed when he pushed off the edge of the countertop with his hips and headed in the direction of the sunroom. But then he spoke again.

"Before I forget, I have something for you."

He was full of surprises tonight…

He disappeared into the other room and returned carrying something wrapped loosely in tissue paper that he brought over to her.

"I asked my grandfather to see if he could fix this and he did…"

Lexie unwrapped the item.

It was the old picture frame that had held the photograph of her grandfather and his new tractor. The frame she'd tried to rehang only to have it fall a second time and break.

Ben Camden had made it good as new.

"I didn't even realize it was missing…" Lexie mused, turning it over and seeing that the repair had made the frame sturdy enough to hold the cherished picture again.

Then she looked up at Micah, at that face that had matured into such rugged glory, into those impossibly blue eyes, and she couldn't deny that it was something sweet and thoughtful for him to have done. It touched her that he had taken the trouble—especially since it wasn't his fault it had broken.

"Thank you," she said softly.

"No big deal. Just keep in mind that you shouldn't hang it back up until all the construction is finished."

Lexie nodded. As she went on looking into

those eyes, she wondered just what kind of man he really was.

If he wasn't the boy she'd known, then who was this guy?

This tall, muscular, gorgeous mountain of a man who was studying her face.

Whose eyes were peering into hers.

Whose gaze drifted to her mouth as if he might be taking aim...

To kiss her?

That couldn't be...

And why would her chin tilt up just a little at that thought?

Certainly, she wouldn't *let* him kiss her.

Would she?

She realized suddenly that she was looking at his lips—such perfect masculine lips.

That parted ever so slightly just then...

And had his handsome head moved a fraction forward, too?

For a moment, she held her breath. She just waited, knowing she should move. That she should deflect.

Only she didn't.

But a split second later, Micah stepped back and away from her.

Nodding at the frame in her hands, he said, "Pops did a good job, but don't forget that it's old. I don't think it can be fixed if it falls and breaks again." For some reason, his voice seemed more gravelly than it had been earlier.

"I'll keep that in mind," Lexie assured him.

"Better get some sleep," he suggested then. "My crew will be here bright and early and you won't be able to sleep through the noise."

"I'll just be glad to get things started."

The repairs to the houses.

Not whatever it was that had seemed on the verge of starting between them.

Unless she'd just imagined it.

Which she probably had.

Because Micah *liking her too much* might have been the case years ago.

But that was ancient history.

And no more welcome now than it would have been then even if she'd known about it.

So why, she asked herself once she got behind her closed bedroom door, was she still thinking about those lips of his?

And why was she just realizing that she'd been a little excited by the idea of him kissing her?

And feeling a hint of disappointment now that he hadn't…

Chapter Six

Wednesday and Thursday were busy days.

The sun was still rising on Wednesday when six burly marine veterans arrived in three pickup trucks and went to work.

As planned, once Lexie was dressed for the day, she went next door to prep the little house for Thursday's tasks. It was a bigger chore than her grandmother's house had been because there was more structural damage to sort through and work around. There was also more damage to possessions, so she had a greater number of things to evaluate as she decided whether to salvage and protect them or dispose of them.

Work was still going on when she finished but she showered the grime away in time to get to Mary's place for dinner.

On Tuesday night, Gertie had suggested that she should leave Micah and his friends to a boys' night and come spend the evening with her and Mary, and Lexie had agreed, staying until Gertie and Mary were ready for bed.

When she got back home, construction had stopped for the night, and Micah and his friends were in the backyard, nearer to the barn than the house. Sleeping bags were still rolled up but ready to use and they were grilling steaks on Gertie's barbecue. It did indeed look like a boys' night on a boisterous camping trip, beer bottles in hand.

The sounds of a whole lot of deep voices and laughter were still drifting up through the window from below when Lexie got into bed. She fell asleep listening hard for which voice, which laugh was Micah's, trying not to analyze why she cared…

She woke Thursday morning to the sound of more power saws and hammering, and spent the day cleaning up the debris the construction had left behind in Gertie's house. The kitchen and her grandmother's bedroom were powdered with sawdust that—despite the plastic sheeting—had also crept onto the stairs and into the living room.

Finished with that late in the afternoon, she

rushed to Mary's apartment to stay with her grandmother while Mary went to the dentist.

"How's the work on the houses going today?" Gertie asked when Lexie brought them both iced teas.

"Good... I think..." Lexie answered uncertainly. "I told you yesterday when I got here that they hadn't really done anything except tear down what was left of the damaged wall. But when I got home last night, all the old stuff was gone and they'd framed the wall in—all nice and neat from the eaves to the ground—and nailed the tarps to it so the tarps don't flap around as much. Now it looks like it's ready for a whole new side wall, though."

"Plastic tarps still aren't locked doors so I'm glad Micah is there making sure nobody comes in," Gertie said.

Lexie nodded rather than agreeing or disagreeing aloud, then went on with what she'd been saying. "Today they're working on my place. The demolition part was finished quicker. The old side was all gone and they'd already started to put up the new frame before I left."

"But they aren't cutting corners, they're doing it right, doing a good job," Gertie said, her tone implying that it was what she assumed to be true.

"It seems like it. Your house has a nice wooden skeleton for the new wall, and Micah said my place would be in the same shape by the time his crew goes home today."

"Poor Micah," Gertie said then. "He has so much to do to get his beer ready for the food festival this weekend—it was bad timing that this was when his friends could get here to work on the houses. But he wouldn't put them off, even though I told him it was all right if he did. Has he been breaking his back working the construction and at the brewery, too?"

It struck Lexie as strange, but in that moment she realized that, unlike before, she wasn't annoyed by Gertie's sympathy for Micah. She also had no inclination to vilify him in response.

Instead, she said, "I didn't know you told him he could put this work off."

"I did."

Okay, he got points for not accepting Gertie's permission to postpone so he could focus on his own interests.

But Lexie didn't tell her grandmother that as she went on to answer Gertie's question. "We haven't even had a full five minutes together since the marines landed, but from what I've seen, I'd say that yes, he is putting in a lot of hours keeping up with both things." And Lexie had seen quite a bit while watching him through every window.

Not to admire how he looked with the tool belt riding low on his hips, of course, but in order to keep tabs on him. To see if he was bailing on the construction to tend to his brewery while other people did the work he'd promised to do.

But that wasn't what she'd seen. He had seemed to check in at the brewery multiple times a day but he'd never stayed long before returning to work alongside the construction crew. If anything was suffering from inattention on his part, it was his brewery, not work on the houses.

"Poor thing," her grandmother repeated.

"He *is* doing a lot of running back and forth," Lexie conceded. "But from what he told me Tuesday night, I guess he was raised for hard work—I just never knew it. Did you?"

"I knew he was a hard worker from when we worked together at the store," Gertie said, obviously not understanding what Lexie was getting at.

"But did you know his mother kind of drove him and his brothers to be competitive and aggressive about every challenge?"

"Raina Camden?"

Lexie didn't think anything Micah had told her about his upbringing had been in confidence. Plus, she knew anything she told her grandmother would never go beyond the two of them. So she told Gertie how Micah was raised.

It came as a surprise to Gertie, too.

"I knew Raina had a bitter side to her," Gertie

said, describing the town's opinion of her as having a chip on her shoulder.

"So that was all she was really known for—her grudges," Lexie mused.

"It was all she ever talked about. She was a pretty woman, caught the eye of half a dozen men. But things never went past one or two dates because all she did on the dates was grouse about the bad hand she'd been dealt in life."

Micah hadn't said his mother was bitter, but the description seemed to fit.

And suddenly something gelled in Lexie's mind.

Micah's mom had been bitter because she'd held on to her grudges. Because she hadn't moved on.

And as much as Lexie recoiled from the thought, it struck her that maybe holding on to her grudge against Micah could be considered bitterness on her part...

Righteous indignation was one thing—and that was always what she'd thought she felt.

But to call it a grudge? To call what she felt bitterness? Those were things she didn't want in her life, coloring who she was and impacting her future.

And now that she had some understanding of what was behind what Micah had done?

As strange as it seemed to her, she found herself thinking that maybe it was time to let it go...

"I'm gonna get more tea—want a refill?" she

asked her grandmother, needing a moment alone with her thoughts.

"No, but if you're getting up I need my afternoon cheesy puffs," Gertie announced.

"I'll get them," Lexie promised, heading for the small apartment's kitchen, taking with her those two ugly words—*grudge* and *bitterness*—and the idea that they might be infecting her...

She definitely didn't want that.

But she also wasn't sure about *not* holding on to what the barn incident had taught her.

Micah *might* be what he claimed he was— changed and matured. But she wasn't absolutely convinced of it. And she still didn't think for a minute that she could trust him.

But what if she stayed cautious and alert while letting go of the resentment, the grudge, the bitterness?

Caution was okay, she decided. Caution wasn't a grudge. It was just learning that with some people she had to be careful. It was just learning a lesson.

On the other hand, she had come home wanting a fresh start. And how could she have a real fresh start if she didn't also work to put the barn incident behind her?

So she had to let go, she decided there and then. The same way she was working to let go of her divorce fallout, she had to let go of her resentments over what Micah had done.

"My cheesy puffs are in the cupboard next to the fridge if you can't find them," Gertie called from the living room.

"Got 'em," Lexie called back, taking the bag and her tea to return to Gertie, and feeling lighter somehow, as if a burden had been lifted from her shoulders.

"Are you getting along better with Micah?" her grandmother asked then.

"I guess you could say we're getting along better."

"*How much* better?" Gertie asked. "Because Tuesday night, Mary and I both thought—"

"We just aren't at each other's throats," Lexie insisted.

"Micah was never at your throat," Gertie pointed out.

"Okay, then I'm not at his throat anymore."

"So progress," Gertie said with satisfaction.

"Sure, I guess," Lexie conceded.

Maybe a little *too* much progress, given that Tuesday night had ended with her thinking he might be on the verge of kissing her...

And worse yet, she *might* have been feeling let down that he hadn't.

"Things are really mixed up for me right now, Gram. I just got divorced, remember?" she said to remind them both. "That throws everything off-kilter. And now I have to deal with Micah, I have to crawl out from under that divorce, I have to get my life restarted, get myself a way to make a living, get my house fixed—believe me, I've got my hands full. If you and Mary are concocting some fantasy that anything is happening between me and Micah, you should forget it because it just isn't possible. I'm in no shape for any kind of new relationship, let alone with *Micah Camden*!"

"Micah isn't a new relationship, he's an old one. And sometimes what was old can be new again…"

"Nope, not happening," Lexie said dismissively.

But secretly she had to admit that in some ways the good parts of their old relationship actually were resurfacing and bringing with them a new twist.

And what if letting go of the past and her grudge and any bitterness made way for more of that new twist? For what might have even started edging toward an attraction to Micah?

She just had to draw the line, she told herself firmly.

She could let go of the past and her grudge and any bitterness, but that was it.

A fresh start definitely didn't mean getting involved with someone from her past.

Especially not with someone from her past who she couldn't trust.

There was nothing—not one single thing—that could or would or should support or encourage an attraction. And so many reasons why an attraction had to be *dis*couraged.

Not the least of which, she told herself, was that his *crush* on her from years ago was history—proven by the fact that he *hadn't* kissed her.

Or even tried to.

So it was cut and dry—nothing was happening between them.

And nothing ever would.

Mary returned from the dentist just then, and she and Gertie tried to persuade Lexie to stay for dinner again.

But Lexie begged off, saying she needed to get home and shower and wash the sawdust out of her hair.

Which was the truth.

And the fact that the marines were leaving, that when she went home, she and Micah would once more have the place to themselves?

She assured herself that that was not a factor.

After all, she'd drawn that line between letting go and attraction.

And she wasn't going to cross it.

As expected, the marines were gone by the time Lexie got home. The side of the little house was framed and ready for a new wall.

She went in the main house's front door, expecting to find Micah inside. Instead, she found a note on the kitchen table telling her he had work to catch up on in the brewery and would be there until late.

Of course, he was behind on his work there, Lexie thought, trying to ignore the deflated feeling she had.

Then it occurred to her that working or not, he still needed to eat. And since it was the construction on her house and her grandmother's house that had put him behind at the brewery, she owed him.

Taking out her cell phone, she texted him that unless he had other plans, she would fix dinner and bring it to him.

He texted back that that sounded great and thanked her.

Lexie felt a small rush of excitement that she told herself was because she was excited to cook.

And she forced herself to believe it.

After showering and fixing her hair and makeup, she again dipped into her new wardrobe to dress, choosing a pair of white capri pants and a lacy white halter top that knotted at her left hip as well as behind her neck.

Sandals finished the look before she went downstairs.

Merritt's generosity had again left Mary and Gertie with more food than they could use so they'd sent her home on Wednesday night with plenty of groceries, including a package of raw chicken breasts, lemons and dry pasta.

Knowing there was cream in the fridge and that Gertie always kept some grated parmesan cheese on hand, too, Lexie set about making lemon chicken alfredo.

While the pasta was boiling and the chicken was sautéing, she put two salads together, made an Italian vinaigrette, baked a baguette of already half-baked bread, sliced it and then made the Alfredo sauce, too.

When everything was done, she took out two cookie sheets to use as trays, loaded them with the food and went out the back door.

She was halfway to the barn/brewery doors when it occurred to her that she could have—and should have—brought only Micah's dinner...

She hadn't said anything in her texts about eating with him. He'd probably planned only to have her bring him a sandwich or something and leave so he could eat *while* he went on working.

And instead, she'd dressed in date clothes, prepared a date-like meal and was on her way with two of everything...

She stopped in her tracks and asked herself what in the world she was doing! And why!

What had she been thinking...

She spun around to return to the house to leave behind her portion, but no sooner was her back to the barn than she heard his deep voice call to her, "Forget something?"

Her sanity? That line she wasn't going to cross?

She slowly pivoted to face the barn again, finding him standing in the open doors.

Standing there with his combat-booted feet apart, his wide shoulders and chest outlined in crisp white knit, she was struck by the undeniable proof of his masculinity. And a simmering sexiness that she did *not* want to be aware of.

Oh, yeah, she'd definitely crossed the line.

He didn't wait for her to answer his question, instead coming toward her, saying as he did, "Let me take those."

Lexie decided to opt for honesty so she said, "For some reason, I brought my dinner, too, and I just realized that I shouldn't have. I'm sure you weren't planning on company. You're probably going to eat while you work. So I was going to take my dinner back and just bring yours."

"No!" he said quickly, taking a tray in each of those big hands. "I don't want you to do that. I can take a break."

The fact that he showed no signs of annoyance did not make Lexie feel any less embarrassed.

"I don't want to bother you. I don't know what I was thinking. You have to be behind."

"But I can take a break," he repeated. "And you're not bothering me. I was glad to get your text. I've been looking forward—" He cut himself off and instead said, "Come on, I'd like you to see the brewery, anyway. Maybe have a taste of the citrus stout at this stage and see if I'm on the right track."

There didn't seem to be a graceful way to decline, so she followed him into the barn-turned-brewery.

Since all the food was covered to stay warm, Lexie opted to leave the trays on the picnic table in a rear corner of the barn, which Micah jokingly called his *break room*, and take the tour first.

The barn was original to the house, but about the only thing that remained from her recollection were the outer walls. The hay loft and stalls were gone, and the floor had been covered with concrete.

Electricity and plumbing had been added and the entire structure had been modernized and sanitized.

As Micah showed her around, he pointed out and explained the use for mash tanks, steam generators, lauter tuns, wort pumps, malt machines, heat exchangers, fermentation tanks, filter tanks, pumps, and cooling and refrigeration equipment.

He outlined his safety measures and the equipment and process for cleaning and sanitation, and told her about the gear used to both bottle and keg his finished products.

And all the while his passion for what he was doing, for the brewery itself was evident.

"Gram always made her home brew in the kitchen," Lexie said when they'd finished the tour. "I had no idea it was this involved to do it on a larger scale."

"Actually I'm a *micro*brewery so this is about as small a scale as it can be done commercially," he informed.

"Good thing it was a big barn," she joked. "And no wonder you had to take investments from your family—this is a really big endeavor."

Seeing it for herself gave Lexie a clearer picture of how serious he had to be about this. Which made it all the more noteworthy that he'd left it to work on the houses with the marines. She felt just a twinge of guilt that couldn't be diffused even by reminding herself that his forklift had done the damage in the first place.

"Before we eat..." he said then, going to one of his tanks and filling a small plastic cup from a spigot. "Taste this and tell me what you think— this is the citrus stout. I haven't done the infusion yet, so keep in mind there'll be more flavor added, but tell me if I have the right balance."

Lexie took a sip and then said, "I'm getting the orange but no tartness," she judged. "I'd say increase the lemon."

"Yeah, I thought it might be a little too sweet. Thanks for the input."

They sat across from each other at the picnic table then and settled in to eat.

He praised her cooking, and then Lexie finally had the chance to get to the news she'd been bursting to share with him.

"Yesterday, I went into the bakery and talked to Nessa Bryant," she announced.

"You did?" he said with just the amount of surprise and enthusiasm she'd hoped for.

"Your information was good—she *does* want to sell and retire." And almost the moment Lexie had stepped into the bakery, the thought of it being hers, of making a career out of it, had felt like the direction she should take. "Nessa said she's put the word out but so far no one has shown any interest—she said I was the first."

"Then there's no one to outbid you if you make an offer."

"We didn't talk price but I did ask her if she might consider carrying the loan. She was on the fence about that. She said she had to talk it over with her husband. But she also said that he still works at the bank and might be able to help me get a loan there if necessary."

"Okay, so you have two options—either she'll decide to carry the loan, or Frank will try extra hard to work it out at the bank for his wife's sake as much as yours," Micah said.

"And if your offer to let me test the market with cupcakes at the food festival is still good—"

"Absolutely," he confirmed.

"Then Nessa said I can use her pans and ovens tomorrow afternoon to make them so I get a feel for the place."

He laughed. "You've been busy. But that's great, too! It'll give you a chance to make sure everything there works the way it should. It'll give you more bargaining power on the price if you know you'll have a big equipment expense going in."

"Good point," Lexie said.

"And what about the rest of the place? I've been in there a few times since I came back but I never looked at it with an eye for making it my business. Did you have any thoughts about what you'd keep the same and what you'd change?"

That she had considered. And as they ate, she told him that the display cases were old but that she thought refinishing them would improve them while keeping their vintage coziness. That she would want to replace the tables and chairs, maybe expand the seating area by making the display windows into window seats because she didn't like Nessa's idea of putting baked goods there and exposing them to the sun and heat.

As for the menu, she'd studied what Nessa was

selling and thought about what she would want to continue to offer, what she might want to omit, what she might want to add.

She went on and on with the thoughts that had been racing through her mind since the day before and Micah listened to it all, making comments, suggestions, encouraging her and showing an interest she hadn't even garnered from Gertie.

"Okay, I'll stop," she said when she realized they'd both finished eating. "I've just gotten really excited about this since yesterday. When I walked in there, it felt meant to be for me."

"I get it. And I'm happy that something has you so inspired. Plus, you know I'm going to take the credit for telling you about Nessa wanting to sell out in the first place," he joked.

"You get full credit for it," she granted. "And thanks for paying enough attention to figure out I might like to own a bakery. And for taking me seriously."

"I didn't really do anything other than listen— to the gossip about Nessa selling and to you talking about enjoying baking. That's not such a big deal," he replied, balking at her gratitude. "Taking you seriously isn't something you need to thank me for, either," he said with a slight frown that showed some confusion.

"You'd be wrong—it is all a big deal. To me, at

least," she said, thinking about her marriage—and about her relationship with Jason overall.

Which led her to something she'd been wondering about since Micah's candor about his adolescent feelings for her. "Did Jason know about your crush all those years ago?" she asked.

"Well…" Micah hedged. "We didn't talk about it. I didn't confess to him or anything. But early on, we were racing to see who could get to you first to walk to the bus stop with you and he'd gloat whenever he won, so that seems like he knew I had the same intentions. In middle school and high school, we had a couple of tussles over you and I being partners in some school projects—he got in my face, said I'd better not forget that you were his. I don't know if he realized feelings were involved or not—he might have just seen it as us competing to be alpha dog…" Micah paused, then said, "But how did we get from being happy about you maybe buying the bakery to *that*?"

"Our talk on Tuesday night just got me to thinking… Jason and my relationship didn't stay the way it started out—the way it was for all those years we were here—"

"And you're wondering if I might have been a factor?"

"Yes. Would he have wanted me the way he did if he hadn't been determined to win out over you?"

"You think the only reason he wanted you was

because he suspected that I did? I don't believe that," Micah said dismissively.

"I don't know… Things between us changed so much after we left here."

"Did things change right away when you left?" Micah asked.

"It wasn't drastic at first, but yes, a little," she said, really thinking about the timeline. "Before we left Merritt, I basically always called the shots—"

"Yeah, I gave him a hard time about that—he followed you around like a puppy. Jill said he was just devoted to you."

"Well, that *definitely* changed," she muttered. "I guess the first time Jason did something that I wasn't on board with was when he dropped out of college six weeks in—he said he needed a break from school, that he'd rather work full-time, save more money for our year of travel, then get his degree when we came back, while I worked."

"That's what you weren't on board with?"

"I would have rather he stuck with our original plan, but his idea sounded reasonable so I went along with it."

"But then you didn't stick college out, either," Micah probed.

"No, I didn't. When my folks were killed, I was a wreck. I just… We were still living here while I commuted to Northbridge for freshman year and Jason worked at the lumbermill, and I wanted to get away from the memories. So when Jason suggested we leave, do our year of travel and then worry about college later—"

"I kind of thought losing your folks was why you took off," Micah contributed.

"It was, at least partially. But once we left," she continued, "what I wanted began to take a real back seat. At first it wasn't as obvious because Jason had already mapped out where we should go, so we just followed that plan—"

"But once you reached the end of that? Of your *year of travel*?"

"That was when we were supposed to come home and go back to college."

"And Jason wasn't ready to do that yet?" Micah said.

"He wasn't. But neither was I…" She sighed. "I still just couldn't deal with the thought of coming back to the memories. So the idea of another year of being footloose and fancy-free—as Jason presented it— of still living day to day and seeing some of the states the way we'd seen Europe… That had more appeal."

"So you went with what Jason wanted because it was basically what you wanted, too."

"Right. But the thing was, I thought I'd have more input on the plan for that."

"And you didn't?"

"He blew off pretty much everything I suggested."

"I can't imagine him blowing off anything with you."

"Like I said, things changed."

"And you didn't put up a fight?" Micah said as if he couldn't believe that.

"I know," Lexie agreed, "it seems strange. I never had any problem speaking up for myself before. But losing my parents left me...I don't know, really vulnerable-feeling, I guess. I had this overwhelming sense that Jason was going to be *it* for me when it came to family... That I'd better make things with him work—that I had to make him happy."

"So you let him call the shots."

It was something she regretted now. Something that had cost her too many years away from her grandmother, away from Merritt and Jill, traveling on an endless journey she wasn't even enjoying because by then Jason had completely stopped taking what she wanted into consideration, and had merely expected her to go on following forever.

"How long were you okay doing what he wanted?" Micah asked.

"Not long," she admitted. "When I could think of my parents again without being miserable, when I started wanting to come home, problems started between us."

"Because Jason still didn't want to come back."

"No. And by then he'd been *in charge* long enough that what I wanted didn't interest him."

"It didn't matter at all?" Micah asked with surprise.

"Things really had changed," she reiterated. "There was a lot of fighting, especially every time I'd say I wanted to come home and settle down—"

"And he never did."

"Nope. And every time I'd just cave," she confessed, feeling the frustrations and anger she'd felt each time.

"That doesn't sound like you, either."

"We were *married*. I kept telling myself that marriages have to have compromise, patience. Jason would swear that he only wanted a little more time away, I'd worry about what it might mean if I *did* push him—"

"And so you'd decide to just do what he wanted again."

Another shrug.

"But here you are without him…"

"Alaska," she said. "That's where we were last winter."

"Winter in Alaska? Don't people go to warmer climates for the winter?"

"Jason thought it would be an interesting experience and I couldn't persuade him otherwise. By that point, it felt as if he deliberately chose to do the opposite of whatever I wanted."

"To prove he had the power? The control?"

"Probably. I was getting too tired of everything— of him—to really care why," Lexie admitted quietly.

"But you went to Alaska."

"Maybe I really needed an extreme to finally get me to face what I needed to face. So we went to Alaska last October. By Christmas, I told Jason that was it for me. I missed Gram, I wasn't spending any more of the time I could be having with her away. I said that after the holidays I was moving back home, with or without him."

"I want to say *finally* but I don't want to make you mad," Micah said cautiously.

"*Finally* is actually fitting. The relationship had been too one-sided for too long and I was *finally* taking back what I'd given over to him."

Micah nodded knowingly, somberly. "One-sided decision-making doesn't work," he said as if he knew it firsthand. But rather than expand on that he encouraged her to go on. "But again, here you are alone…divorced…"

"When I told Jason, he thought he had a bargaining chip—we were both working at a hotel in Anchorage—me in the restaurant, him at the front desk. He told me he'd been having an affair with the concierge—"

"*That* was a bargaining chip?"

"He said he'd break it off and we could move again, but if he did that for me, I had to agree not to move back to Merritt."

"Oh, jeez," Micah said in disbelief.

"That was when I realized just how little I really had come to mean to him… And frankly, how little I cared about being with him anymore. No matter the place."

"Wow. I just can't picture it going so wrong…" Micah marveled.

"Because the relationship was so different before, when he wanted to beat you by being with me," she said, returning to what had begun this. "Now I have to wonder how much of a part the competition between the two of you played in our relationship—whether it would have happened at all if he hadn't been so intent on *winning*."

Micah's only response was a questioning arch of his eyebrows.

"I just have to wonder," she went on, "if the competition hadn't been at play, would he have tried so hard with me in middle school or high school, would he have put so much effort into pleasing me or would he have shown his true colors—because that's what I think really came out after we left town."

"I'm sorry if that was the case," Micah said, sounding genuinely contrite. "But one way or another, Jason didn't have the right to run you around the way he did, to cheat on you."

Micah reached across the table and covered her hand with his. "As far as I'm concerned, cheating is a lowlife move no matter what. But if it makes you feel better to blame me and the competition—"

That actually caused her to laugh. "You'll just be the catch-all for every lousy thing that's happened?"

He shrugged those glorious shoulders that did look broad and strong enough to bear the weight.

"No, you don't get the blame for Jason's bad behavior. He can carry that on his own," she said, trying not to nestle her hand even deeper into Micah's.

He squeezed and then let go, retrieving his hand as if he weren't sure if *he* might have crossed a line by touching her.

"So if that all happened at Christmas, why did you stay in Alaska through the rest of the winter?" he asked.

"I didn't want being in different states to complicate—or delay—the divorce. Because I stayed and did it there, and because we didn't have any property to divide, it only took thirty days. Once it was over, though, I still couldn't leave right away. I'd gotten to be friends with my boss, Lily. She'd helped me through the whole thing and had three waitresses going out on maternity leave, so I didn't want to jump ship when she needed me most. But I was set to come home two weeks from when Mary called about Gram."

"I'm sorry, Lexie, that it all went the way it did," Micah said then. "I'm sorry you got hurt—I never would have thought you were in line for that with Jason."

"I never would have thought that, either."

It struck Lexie then that she'd been talking for much longer than she'd intended.

"I didn't mean to keep you from your work so long!" she said, standing up and beginning to re-load the cookie sheets with the remnants of their dinner.

"No complaints," he said. "As far as I'm concerned, you can stay all night—I'd be happy for the company…"

She was sure he was just being nice.

"No, I'll get out of here and let you go back to what you need to be doing."

But once the cookie sheets were reloaded, Micah reached for them before she could, picking up both of them. "I'll carry these over to the house, help you clean up."

"I cleaned as I cooked so there are only these few dishes. I'll take care of them. And I can carry "

"Come on," was all he said as he headed out of the brewery.

On the way across the yard, he nodded in the direction of the newly framed wall. "You haven't told me what you think about the work on the houses."

"It looks good," she said, still fighting embarrassment for having overshared and eaten up his evening.

When they got to the house, she moved in front of him to open the door, holding it for him and then following him into the kitchen.

"Were we too rowdy last night?" he asked as he set the trays near the kitchen sink. "Did we keep you up?"

Why did it sound as if he were just searching for an excuse to linger? Surely he'd already lost more time than he should have and needed—wanted—to get back. Didn't he?

But he'd asked questions it would be rude to ignore, so she said, "No, you didn't bother me." And she could have left it at that. But since he propped a hip against the edge of the counter and seemed in no hurry to leave, she did the same thing, facing him, and said, "It seemed like you had a good time. Are you friends with all those guys?"

"Some of them. Some I just met when they got here."

"I would never have guessed that—I thought you were all buddies. It *looked* like you were…"

"We're all vets. Most of that crew were marines but the branch of service doesn't matter. The military is a brotherhood—there's a bond even among strangers who have served."

Seeing what she'd seen had left her curious. "You were so…one of the guys. So relaxed. Years ago, you were constantly horsing around, wrestling, playing keep-away, elbowing your way to the front of lines, vying for something or another—"

"That was the whole competing thing," he said.

"But from what I saw last night, you weren't anything like that," she observed, recalling the comradery she'd witnessed. "You're so much more calm now. Comfortable in your own skin—or at least that's how it seems…" Strong, confident, certain of his own power. It was all different from the Micah she remembered—but it was also potently attractive, especially for the way it made her consider more seriously the idea that he really might have changed.

"It's like you don't have anything to prove anymore," she said.

"I have to prove I can make good beer," he responded with a laugh, stretching his right arm out to lay his hand on the countertop not far from where she was. Then he returned to the subject of the repairs. "It looks like most of the crew will be able to come back for another two days next week to get the walls up. We'll be tarp-free when that happens."

So more days when he'd be otherwise occupied, when she would barely see him, when they wouldn't have evenings like this one...

Lexie nodded, reminding herself that she and Gertie needed the work done. That mattered much more than the ridiculous internal voice saying that she'd missed him...

"Can you spare more time away from the brewery?" she asked.

"Can or can't, I will," he said. "I promised you and Gertie I'd get this mess fixed as soon as possible. Besides, it's to my benefit to make sure everything is up to code so we don't have any problems with the inspections."

She nodded a second time and something else occurred to her suddenly—if the houses were securely walled again, there wouldn't be a need for him to stay in the sunroom...

And that thought didn't sit well, either.

Although it certainly *should* have.

"I suppose when the walls are up, you'll be able to go home..." she said, testing the waters.

He grinned a mischievous grin that made his blue eyes sparkle as they stayed raptly on her. "Will you be sorry to see me go?" he joked.

He was obviously kidding—but that didn't make it any less true. She didn't know how or when it had happened, but she didn't want him to go.

"I might be just a little sorry..." she heard herself admit before she realized she was going to. Then backtracking, she added, "I've never stayed out here—in the country, at the farm—alone."

"If it helps, I can stay," he offered. "It's easier for me to be closer to the brewery."

"Then you could make up a little of the time you lose working on the houses," she reasoned, even though she knew, knew, knew that she should be eager for him to go.

He seemed as surprised by her words as she was herself, looking at her so intently, so quizzically.

"Are we on better terms than we were?" he asked her flat out.

They'd been on horrible terms before. Admitting to a small improvement didn't seem too bad. It didn't mean she had to admit to the attraction that was becoming harder and harder for her to deny.

So she said, "Maybe. A little."

His well-sculpted face erupted in a smile that was pleased, relieved and oh-so-sexy.

Damn him...

"Are we friends again?" he asked.

"I don't know if I'd go that far."

He didn't seem to buy that phony aloofness because his smile turned into a devilish grin. "Okay..." he said, with mock confusion. "Then what are we?"

Good question...

"I don't know," Lexie answered.

She also didn't know why her voice had gone

quiet. Or why she kept looking up into those mesmerizing ultra-blue eyes.

"Maybe we're getting to be more than friends..." Micah suggested, his deep voice almost a whisper.

She knew she should stomp on that idea before it sprouted any roots.

But somewhere along the way he'd come closer and all she could think about was Tuesday night when she'd been half ready for him to kiss her.

Tuesday night when he hadn't, and she'd come away disappointed.

She'd been thinking about him kissing her almost every minute since then.

Wondering what it might have been like. What it might *be* like.

Wanting to know despite every argument she'd had with herself against it...

Now he was leaning in by infinitesimal increments. So slowly that there was lots of opportunity for her to call a halt to it or back up.

But there she was, holding her ground. Almost daring him to do it.

This guy who she knew never turned down a dare...

His mouth was so near hers. So near but not touching—yet.

And she couldn't take it anymore.

Without another thought, she kissed him.

A little laugh rumbled in his throat just before he took over, kissing her for the first time.

And whoa, what a kiss!

Never had she been kissed like that.

There was special talent in those amazingly adept lips. Lips that met hers with just the right amount of pressure and command, just the right amount of softness and allure, parted just enough to entice and tempt and promise more.

That big hand that had been resting on the counter rose to the back of her head. His long fingers combed through her hair, pulling her just slightly closer. It felt so good that there was just no way Lexie could keep from losing herself in it all.

She kissed him back with a kind of hunger she'd never experienced with her ex. A kind of hunger she hadn't known she was capable of feeling.

Which was a bit alarming.

And a little voice in the back of her mind suddenly shrieked, *What are you doing?*

This is Micah Camden!

This can't happen!

This has to stop!

And yet it went on for a few moments longer because she just couldn't bring herself to end a kiss that good.

Until she finally forced herself to, pulling out of it.

"We can't do this," she muttered, hating that she sounded so breathless.

"We can't?" he challenged.

"No," she said firmly, offering no reason but finally looking him in the eye again to meet his challenge.

His eyebrows rose once more as if he were tempted to argue. But he didn't.

"Okay," he said.

He took his hand from behind her head and stepped back. But he went on looking at her.

Then, as if hoping she would argue, he said, "I better get to work."

Lexie confirmed that with another nod.

Still, he studied her face for a moment more before what looked like marine discipline came over him and he was suddenly all business.

And for some reason she was sorry to see that.

"Text me how much stout you need for your cupcakes and I'll bring it over so you'll have it to take with you to the bakery tomorrow," he said.

She'd forgotten about that. "Oh…sure… I'll need to increase the recipe. Once I do the math, I'll let you know."

"It'll be in the fridge," he promised, his gaze staying with her another minute before he broke the connection, turned and went out the back door.

As she watched him go, Lexie told herself that

she hadn't just crossed the line, she'd leaped over it. Bounded over it. Left it far behind.

And she shouldn't have.

You can't let that ever happen again, she warned herself, going over in her mind all the reasons why—she was only months out of her marriage; this was *Micah* and even if she'd let go of old resentments for the barn incident, she still shouldn't trust him; she needed all of her focus and energy put into her fresh start before she even contemplated getting into a relationship again.

But no matter how much she tried, she couldn't wipe away the memory of that kiss.

And she also couldn't deny how very—very— much she'd liked it...

Chapter Seven

"Oh, man, that's good beer!"

"That's what I'm going for," Micah said, pleased with his brother Tanner's praise for the bottle of oat stout he'd offered when Tanner came to the brewery Friday afternoon.

Micah had shown his younger brother around and—like the night before with Lexie—they'd ended up sitting at the picnic table together.

"How did you do all this in just the six months since you resigned your commission?" Tanner asked with some amazement.

"Workin' day and night," Micah confirmed. "But you know I've been experimenting with the hops and the beer itself for years. This has all just been putting everything into play on a bigger scale."

"And you're launching at the food festival tomorrow night—I'm impressed," Tanner said.

"I don't know if the food festival can be called a launch, but it will be the first time the three plain stouts will be for sale. Once I get the flavored stouts right, the Denver cousins will give me a real launch with the plain stouts in the Camden Superstores."

"I had a layover in Denver on my way here, spent the night at GiGi's house. She had a big family dinner and everybody was talking about you and your beer. They're all excited about it."

"Nice," Micah said before solemnly adding, "I hope to God I don't disappoint them."

For years, their mother's resentment of the Denver Camdens had kept them away from their cousins. Their grandfather had never given up lobbying for a connection, though. Ben had finally struck pay dirt when he'd pointed out that if her sons had a relationship with their successful cousins, the drive for all that success might inspire them to work even harder. Raina had seen some logic in that and had finally conceded.

As a result, when Micah and the triplets were just entering their teens, they'd begun the ritual of long summer visits with the Denver cousins. During those annual trips, they'd forged strong family ties with all ten of their cousins, and had also grown fond of the cousins' grandmother, GiGi. In fact, they'd come to think of GiGi Camden as a surrogate grandmother.

Tanner took another drink of his beer, then said, "They won't be disappointed with this."

"I'll send a case home with you—Pops likes the rye stout better so I keep him stocked in that." Micah paused and then segued into what he and their grandfather were curious about. "Shall I send you with two cases? Will you be around long enough to drink more?"

Tanner stared at the label on the bottle in his hand. "I don't know," he said. His tone made it clear that something was weighing on him.

"How long is your leave?"

"I have thirty days coming, if I need to take them."

"If you *need* to take them..."

Tanner didn't say anything to that.

Micah decided to push his brother a little to see if he could get to the bottom of whatever was on Tanner's mind. "Are you okay?"

"I'm fine," Tanner assured him.

"But you *needed* to take a leave and come all the way here?"

To Micah's frustration, Tanner dodged the question, saying, "You've been home six months—what do you know about Della Markham?"

Micah hadn't expected that. "Your old high school sweetheart? I know she died two months ago in childbirth—even though I hadn't realized that still happened these days outside of third world countries."

The rarity of it had caused it to be widely talked about around town. That was the only reason he'd really been aware of it.

But why would that have brought Tanner home on sudden leave?

"I met your old buddy Nate McAdams in a bar a couple of weeks ago," Tanner said then.

Micah nodded his understanding. Nate had become an architect like his dad. He worked out of the office in Merritt, but Micah had heard that most of their business was somewhere else.

"He was in Iran building a house for a sheikh, if you can believe it," Tanner continued. "We had a drink. He was telling me all the news from Merritt. The news about Della was the biggest."

Big enough to bring Tanner home?

"Had you kept in contact with Della all these years? Even after…" After the enormous ruckus she'd caused that had almost derailed Tanner's whole future?

"No, but I did run into her when I was home last time. We had coffee," Tanner admitted. "What do you know about the baby? About the father of the baby?"

"Nothing much," Micah answered. "I've been deep into getting the brewery up and running. Della dying when she gave birth was the first time I'd heard anything about her since I got back. That was…I don't know, I guess two months ago? Part of the gossip was about how nobody knew who the father was. I guess she'd kept it under wraps the whole time she was pregnant. People were figuring the father was married."

"That *would* make sense…" Tanner said, sounding surprised. "But nobody stepped up—married or not—to claim the baby?"

"No. Actually that was what made folks believe it *was* a married man who was hiding the affair— and that he figured he could keep his wife from ever knowing what he'd done as long as he kept his mouth shut."

"McAdams said Della's sister took it?"

"If I'm remembering right, *it* was a girl, and yeah, I heard something about a sister taking her… I didn't even remember there *was* a sister," Micah said.

"Addie. She was a lot younger," Tanner informed. "I think she was like…eleven or twelve when Della and I graduated…"

"But grown up now so she could take on her niece," Micah concluded.

"McAdams said she's still in town. With the baby."

Micah shrugged. "I honestly don't know anything about that. The only thing I know for sure is that Della died. The rest is just what I recall hearing—but I can't claim I was listening all that closely," Micah said, his curiosity about Tanner's interest only getting bigger by the minute. "You want to tell me why any of it matters to you?" he ventured, finally being direct.

"No," his brother answered flatly.

Micah wondered if it was possible that Tanner had retained a soft spot for his old girlfriend. Maybe he'd come home to pay respects, maybe to make sure the infant she'd left behind was cared for.

Or maybe there was more going on than his brother was telling him.

Part of Micah wanted to force the information out of Tanner, the way he would have when they were kids.

But they were both grown men now.

And how could Micah fault his brother for not wanting to share when Micah also didn't want to talk about what was on his own mind today?

So all he said was, "I'm here for you, if there's anything I can do."

"Thanks," Tanner said. Then he changed the topic with a nod in the direction of Gertie's house.

"How about you? How are you doin' over here with Lexie after everything?"

The triplets had only been a year behind Micah in school so they'd known the whole barn story—including all the fallout.

"It started out bad," Micah answered honestly.

"I'm not surprised. She really had it in for you."

"Not without cause."

"Yeah, what you did was pretty uncool," Tanner said with a sympathetic laugh. "But you wanted her like nothing I've ever seen and you know how we were raised…"

"Definitely not cool." All the way around.

"And now Pops says you did that damage to the houses?"

"Not personally, but yeah, it happened because of me…"

"That couldn't have helped things."

"Nope."

"So she still wants your head on a platter?" The amusement Tanner found in that idea seemed to lighten his own concerns.

"I think things are smoothing out." Although he didn't know if that kiss the night before might have roughed them up again. Especially since she'd left this morning before he'd had the chance to see her or talk to her.

"How smooth are they getting?" his brother asked with a hint of innuendo.

"Not *that* smooth," Micah shot back. "We've had some good talks. She's pinch-hitting for Gertie while Gertie is laid up, helping me get the levels right in the flavored stouts. I steered her toward maybe buying the bakery from Nessa Bryant and offered to share my booth at the food festival with her—she's making cupcakes with my stout in them to see what kind of reception her stuff gets. I'd say that we're not doing too bad. But the past casts a shadow…"

To Micah that had all sounded neutral but it seemed to spark some instinct in Tanner because he said more solemnly, "You got over her, didn't you? I mean, there's been a steady stream of the female persuasion in your life—most recently Adrianna, right? That was even serious. It isn't as if you've been carrying a torch or something. Or have you been hiding it all this time?"

"You've just shown up here out of the blue because of your old girlfriend—I could ask you the same thing," Micah countered.

His brother got the message to let the subject drop. "Fair enough," he said with a slight laugh, backing off much the way Micah had with him. "If there's anything *I* can do…" he returned the offer.

"Thanks."

Tanner finished his stout and set the bottle on the table. Then he pushed himself to his feet. "Big Ben sent me with a list of errands to run in town.

You have any you need me to handle while I'm there?"

Micah didn't.

"Then I better get going. Thanks for the beer. And don't forget my case."

Micah got up, went to the cooler and returned with the promised supply of stout.

"I'll let you know if and when I need another," his brother said. "It's good stuff, might be sooner rather than later."

"Just holler."

He walked his brother to the barn door where they said goodbye.

Micah should have returned to work then. But instead, he leaned a shoulder against the door frame, staring at the back of Gertie's house long after Tanner had driven away.

Catching a glimpse of Lexie was usually the reason he looked over at the house, but he knew she was gone. Right now, it was just that she was on his mind. On top of the bigger issue that was dogging him today.

He *had* gotten over her—that was the answer to Tanner's question. He had *not* been carrying a torch for her.

It hadn't happened instantly, back in high school. But it *had* happened. Time, growing up, moving on to other things, other attractions, other relationships, had all taken care of it.

Sure, he'd thought about her here and there but it hadn't been to pine for her, but to grapple with his shame for what he'd done. Shame that, it turned out, was a fairly decent antidote for a crush.

What his brother hadn't guessed was that something new had begun since her return. Something more than a crush. Yes, he was back to thinking about her all the time, noticing every detail, wanting to be with her. All that was just the same as it had been when they were kids.

But there was also something that went beyond the schoolboy crush to something deeper in him. Something that was getting increasingly harder to fight. Something that was even defeating the marine discipline that had become fundamental to him.

It was why he'd nearly kissed her on Tuesday night. It was why he'd been on the verge of kissing her last night.

And the fact that it had actually been Lexie who had kissed him when he'd been trying to talk himself out of kissing her?

That sure as hell hadn't helped matters. In fact, the surprise of that had sapped all the fight out of him.

She'd kissed *him*...

And he couldn't stop wondering why. Could it be that something was coming to life in her, too?

If there might actually be something *mutual* happening this time...

That was a dangerous thought.

Especially when he knew what he was dealing with.

She was half a step out of a marriage. A marriage to her first love. The only person—as far as he knew—who she'd ever kissed before, who she'd ever been with.

To kiss him now, at her own instigation, shouted *rebound* to him. It seemed all too likely that she was experimenting just to see what it was like to kiss someone else—*anyone* else.

So she'd kissed him.

But probably only because he'd been there at the time. And because he'd been inviting it.

Rebounding, testing her wings, experimenting—that was basic and superficial. That was Lexie going backward to do what most everyone did in their teens, what she hadn't done because she'd coupled with Jason when they were both kids and hadn't uncoupled until just now. That was Lexie needing to try everything she should have tried long ago.

Yeah, that had to be what it was.

And as much as he would have liked to convince himself there was more to it, he couldn't let himself get carried away. Instead, he had to keep his wits about him. Keep from reading more into anything she did than was really there.

The bottom line, he decided, was that they were once again on different pages.

Years ago, he'd been obsessed with her and she'd seen him simply as a friend.

Now she saw him as someone to practice on to get her feet wet again, while he was afraid that one flip of a switch and he could be into more serious feelings for her.

But only a fool would let himself fall for a woman who had no intention of loving him back.

And he wasn't a fool.

But damn if it wouldn't have been a whole lot easier if she *hadn't* kissed him last night.

Because as much as he'd wanted to kiss her, he'd never expected kissing her to be like that.

Kissing her had been better than he'd ever imagined—and he'd imagined it a *lot*.

It had knocked him for a loop more than kissing anyone ever had.

But he needed to keep his feet firmly planted on the ground.

The last time he'd been knocked for a loop was painfully vivid in his mind, and the memory of it had been tormenting him since he'd opened his eyes to this particular day.

So he was going to take a giant step back from Lexie, he decided. Yes, they were living in the same house and he needed her to help with his flavored stouts, but mentally, emotionally, he was withdrawing.

Back to where he hadn't lost sight of the true nature of things between them.

Back to where he hadn't been thinking about her every minute—or at all.

Back to where he wasn't haunted by the image of her.

Back to where kissing her wasn't so much a thought, let alone an option.

Romance between them just wasn't meant to be. He'd accepted that once. He was accepting it again now.

Regardless of how incredible that kiss had been.

And never was there a better day than this to remind him that good did not come out of the shadows cast by his own self-absorption. Not with Lexie. Not with Adrianna.

"So open your eyes and keep them open," he muttered to himself, determined to stop playing with fire when it came to Lexie.

"Hi…"

It was after ten o'clock by the time Lexie got home Friday night. When she went in, she found Micah sitting at the kitchen table.

His elbows and forearms were on the oak top, both big hands wrapped around a bottle of beer, and he was staring at that bottle, so lost in his own thoughts that he didn't seem to have heard her entrance.

Her greeting was tentative, since she was uncertain about disturbing him.

His head yanked up in surprise at her voice, and he turned in her direction as he sat straighter in the chair. "Hi," he said in response. "You're just getting home?"

"I am," she answered.

"Long day or did you go to see Gertie tonight?" he asked, pivoting in the chair to face her.

"I saw Gram before I went to the bakery this morning."

"How's she doing?"

"She feels good, and she and Mary always have something going on—this afternoon it was quilting and tonight it was a potluck supper at the apartment."

Micah nodded but didn't say anything.

Something seemed off with him. Ordinarily he gave the impression of having the strength and energy of ten men.

But tonight, he seemed drained in a way she'd never seen before.

Maybe he was tired? Or sick? Or had gotten some bad news?

"Are you okay?" she asked.

"Sure," he answered listlessly. "Are you?"

"I am," she said a second time, determinedly

cheerful. But thinking about ill-health, she said, "Did you know that Nessa decided to retire and sell the bakery because she's not well?"

Micah shook his head.

"When I got there today, she was in bad shape—I guess she has arthritis in her hands and knees. Neither of the girls who work for her were scheduled or could come in on short notice so I offered to run things."

"Did she let you?"

"She did—I think she was so miserable she just wanted to go home."

"So you ran the bakery today?" he said with a faint hint of his usual excitement.

"I did. But since I was on my own that meant I couldn't really do anything but prep for my cupcakes between customers. I couldn't mix or bake until after closing so I had to stay late."

He chuckled half-heartedly. "Welcome to owning your own business. Did it change your mind about buying her out?"

"No. It was a good day, just a long one. And it let me know that business is booming."

"Great," he said as if he were trying—and failing—to rally.

Maybe he'd had a bad day?

"How was your day?" she asked, fishing.

"Fine. I did the citrus infusion…maybe tomorrow you can give it a taste?"

"I can taste it now if you want."

"Yeah, I was going to bring a sample but then I forgot and everything is closed up now... So tomorrow?"

"Sure," Lexie said, more certain than ever that something was on his mind if he'd been distracted from his beer making.

She held up the pink bakery box she'd brought in with her and said, "Nessa said I could leave my cupcakes there—it'll be easier to get them from the bakery to the festival tomorrow—but I brought a few home. I thought you might want to try one..."

"I do. But I worked until about half an hour ago, too. I should probably eat something else first. Did you have dinner?"

"No time. I was going to make a sandwich now. How about I make two?" she suggested.

"I should shower..." he said, sounding unenthused about moving.

"Okay, shower while I make sandwiches. And it's stuffy in here and I was cooped up all day and night—how about if we eat outside?"

"Yeah, sure, whatever you want..." Another lackluster response before he got up and left.

Instantly, Lexie began to worry that his dark mood was because of that kiss last night.

Had she misread the signs? Maybe he hadn't been about to kiss her. And if that were the case and she'd just jumped him...

Maybe he was struggling with the need to tell her she shouldn't have. To tell her that that wasn't something he wanted. To tell her never to do that again.

Oh, that would be awkward and so, so embarrassing…

That kiss had been on her mind all day.

It had been so incredibly good.

And bad…

Bad for her peace of mind, that is. The kiss itself had been so good she just wanted to do it again.

No, she didn't *just* want to do it again; she'd been itching to do it again. Craving it. Wondering desperately if there was any chance of doing it again.

But on the other hand, she knew she shouldn't be fixated on repeating something she'd already decided could *not* happen a second time. Something that never should have happened a first time.

And yet no matter how often she'd reminded herself *why* it shouldn't have happened and couldn't happen again, she'd kept circling around to that yearning for more.

Only now was she realizing that she might have made a huge faux pas. That Micah might not have wanted to kiss her. That she might have come home to find him struggling to find a way to tell her…

She wanted to slink away into the night.

But what good would that do? She would still have to face him eventually. And if he needed to talk to her about it, better to get it over with.

Maybe she should beat him to the punch. Tell him it should never have happened. Maybe apologize? Assure him it would never happen again. Would it be less awkward and uncomfortable if she said it than if he did?

Since she'd been the one to kiss him, she thought it should come from her. So as she gathered the ingredients and began to make two sandwiches, she started to rehearse in her mind what to say, how to say it.

She couldn't come up with any way that didn't seem humiliating.

What had she thought—that just because he'd had a crush on her when they were kids that he still wanted her now? Had she only imagined that he'd been moving in to kiss her? Was that just what she'd needed to think because she'd wanted so badly to kiss him?

Was she just completely clueless when it came to this whole being single thing?

There was no question about it—she was definitely clueless when it came to that.

But still…

Yes, she'd ended up initiating that kiss but the minute she had, he'd run with it—she hadn't imagined that! She hadn't imagined his hand in her hair, holding her to the kiss that *he* had escalated.

Then it occurred to her that just because she'd been immersed in thoughts of that kiss since it happened didn't mean it had been a big deal to him.

In fact, there was no reason to think it had meant anything to him at all…

But if he wasn't bothered by that kiss, then what was wrong with him tonight?

By the time she'd finished making the sandwiches, put them on plates with chips on the side and loaded a cookie sheet to use as a tray again, she didn't know what to do.

Once she'd carried everything outside, she had two options for where they should eat—at the picnic table again or at the more intimate firepit…

Picnic table, she told herself.

But the semi-circular sofa was so much more inviting and comfy…

Long day, she deserved comfy…

So to the firepit she went, leaving it covered so it could act as the table for their food.

With her mind still spinning, Lexie sat just off-center on the outdoor sofa, settling in place a moment before Micah came out.

"This is nice," he commented as he joined her, sitting close by because the small sofa only provided so much room.

She could smell the clean scent of his soap but she tried not to like it.

He was dressed in his gray sweats. His hair was still damp. And his scruff of beard was freshly trimmed. But there was still a solemn air about him even though he smiled and thanked her for making the sandwiches.

So when they'd both taken their plates on their laps and settled into eating, Lexie decided to do more probing and said, "Did something go wrong with your flavored stouts?"

"No, why?" he asked, sounding surprised.

She finally chose to just be blunt. "I'm trying to figure out what's going on tonight. Since I got back to Merritt, you've been...I don't know...gung ho, upbeat, full steam ahead. But tonight, you look like you lost your best friend..."

"Do I? I'm sorry, I didn't mean to be a drag."

"You don't have to be sorry. I'm just wondering what's wrong. Have you had bad news?"

"Nah," he said, taking a bite of his sandwich.

"I don't mean to pry. Is it something you don't want to talk about?" she asked because he didn't offer more than that.

He seemed to use the time it took to eat his bite to consider that, following it up with a swig of the beer he'd brought out with him.

Then, rather than setting the bottle down he raised it in what appeared to be a mock toast and said, "Today is the day I could have become a father. And I've been carrying that thought around with me since I woke up this morning. I guess it's got me down. That thought and the reason for why I'm not." He took another mouthful of beer.

Lexie was so stunned she nearly choked. Sputtering, she pressed a hand to her sternum and took a drink of water.

"Are you all right?" he asked.

She nodded but bought herself another moment by drinking more water.

As she did, she recalled a comment Micah had made several days ago that had seemed odd to her at the time.

After her day with Jill's family, she'd joked about it not seeming like they were all old enough to have kids. She remembered that there had been an unusual seriousness to his confirmation that they were. Was this part of that?

She was too startled to do anything more than repeat what he'd said. "Today is the day you could have become a *father*?"

"It was the due date."

Still stunned, it struck Lexie that since she'd returned to their home town her thoughts about Micah had revolved around their issues—the barn scandal of their past, her anger over the damage to the houses, even her jealousy over his closeness to Gertie.

Nowhere in any of it had she considered his personal life. The *women* in his life.

But, of course, there had been women in his life. Look at him—there were probably hordes of them clamoring after him. And for all she knew, there could be one special woman he was involved with right now. Someone she just hadn't crossed paths with yet…

Lexie drank more water as if it might wash away the weird feelings that were rising in her at the thought of Micah and another woman.

Weird feelings that seemed like jealousy…

It was all very confusing…

"Were you married? *Are* you married?" Lexie said, trying to sort through things. Given how little she'd kept up with his life, anything was possible.

"Am I *married*? Do you think if I was married that wouldn't have come up by now?"

"I don't know. It just this minute occurred to me that I haven't thought about you and…*women*…"

A bemused frown came across his handsome face.

"I know, it doesn't make sense," Lexie said in response. "I know there have to have been women in your life. I just…haven't thought about it…"

"There *have* been women in my life."

"A lot of them?" she heard herself ask.

"My fair share."

"Women you were serious about?"

He didn't answer that in any hurry. Then he said, "I have only been serious about the Marines and getting my brewery built."

"Were there women who were serious about you?" she asked, taking a different tack.

"I was always up-front with anybody I started to see more than a time or two. I made it clear that as long as I was a marine and until I had my brewery up and running, I wasn't interested in anything long-term. I didn't want to mislead anyone."

Lexie knew that was his way of saying he'd learned his lesson with the barn incident and changed his ways.

"But yeah, there were a couple of women who started thinking they could change my mind."

"Was the woman who got pregnant one of them?"

"I'm not sure," he said with another frown, this one dark. "I didn't think so but... I don't know..." He sighed. "Her name is Adrianna. She's a nurse I met when a buddy got hurt in a training maneuver. She worked in the veterans hospital in San Diego, so she understood what it was like to get hooked up with somebody in the military. She was patient about deployments, missions, assignments. And she had her career to concentrate on, so she didn't want anything serious, either."

"How long were you together?"

"Together..." he parroted. "Kind of hard to call it that when one person is stationary and the other

is just in and out… We started seeing each other about…I don't know, I guess about two years ago."

"Exclusively?"

"I never juggled women," he said resolutely. "That's something you can take credit for—I heard what you had to say about guys in school who did that, and those words stuck with me. But yes, we had that conversation about a year ago and agreed to be exclusive."

"But there still wasn't talk of the *long-term*?"

"No," he said.

Lexie merely nodded, wondering if the woman truly hadn't wanted more—or had just known better than to ask for it.

"And then this woman got pregnant?" Lexie asked.

"First, she came here to take care of Mom at the end."

"From San Diego?"

"She was looking to make a job change, thinking that she might like to become a hospice nurse. She had a lot of vacation time coming, Mom was in a big decline and hospice had been recommended, so Adrianna offered to come here and stay. She said it would be a trial run to see if it was a change she really wanted to make—two birds with one stone. And my brothers and I paid her what we would have paid any private nurse."

"So it didn't seem like she was doing it because

she was more invested than you in the relationship—it seemed career-motivated," Lexie said.

"Right. I came home on leave about the same time Adrianna got here to help get her settled in, and to introduce her to Mom and Big Ben. I had a three-day leave, then I had to go back on duty, so we had three days together—"

"And you found a way to get some privacy..." Lexie filled in.

"And six weeks later, Adrianna called, told me the doctor didn't think Mom had more than a few days left, that I should put in for emergency leave. And that she—Adrianna—was pregnant..."

"That was a double whammy."

"At that point, I was talking to Adrianna almost every day on the phone for an update on Mom, so I knew she was failing—that didn't come as a shock. But the pregnancy news... I wasn't expecting that..."

"I imagine it was like a bomb dropping," Lexie suggested.

"Oh, yeah..." he muttered as if experiencing the shock all over again. "I had to get my bearings. In the moment, all I said was that we'd talk when I got home. That was where we left it."

He'd finished his sandwich and chips and set his plate on the firepit. When he sat back again, he was more angled toward her.

"I put in for emergency leave," he went on. "And

while I was waiting for that, I did a lot of thinking. Marriage wasn't in my plans, but if there was going to be a baby… I decided I was going to propose as soon as I got home—"

"Even though you didn't love her?"

Micah sighed. "You're right that I didn't love her. But I had feelings for her. I cared about her. And there was going to be a kid. *My* kid. I knew Adrianna was a decent person. I was going to make the best of it. I *would* have made the best of it."

He said that with so much conviction that Lexie didn't doubt him. He would have done his best to make the marriage work.

"Mom died before I could get back," he continued. "I got in the morning of the funeral. You can't propose at a funeral. I figured I'd wait for the dust to settle, then ask Adrianna to marry me."

His expression went dark. "Before I had the chance, Adrianna had her bags packed. She got me alone and said that she'd had the pregnancy terminated—and that she and I were done."

"Oh," Lexie said in surprise. "I was thinking that you might have been wrong about her, that maybe she did want something long-term, and was playing a waiting game until you got on the same page."

"You're not wrong. There was a waiting game—but it was one that my mother had changed. Adrianna said that when I didn't seem thrilled with the news, she started thinking back to what Mom had said while she'd been taking care of her. I guess Mom had talked about how proud she was of her sons for how we'd turned out, for how much we'd taken to heart what she'd tried to teach us about not letting anything or anyone stand in our way. Adrianna said she'd looked at our relationship, and how my priorities had been Marines first, the beer making and brewery plans second, and her a distant third."

"But that was how you'd laid it out from the beginning," Lexie said in his defense.

He nodded his agreement but it didn't seem to console him. "Adrianna said she'd been kidding herself, thinking things might be different with her and that I might change my mind about commitment. But after listening to what Mom had to say and reevaluating how things had been between us, she'd decided she'd never be my priority—and she didn't believe a baby would be, either. I was just too into my own stuff…" he finished, his voice filled with sorrow.

"That seems a little premature, though," Lexie felt compelled to say in his defense again. "It was a surprise when you got the news. A shock. Didn't she think she should give you a minute to let it sink in and *then* judge your reaction?"

"She said she didn't think she should bother," he said as if repeating his ex's argument.

"But it seems like she should have at least talked to you about ending a pregnancy before she did it," Lexie said quietly. "She should have given you the chance…a say…in the decision."

"Yeah, I did a lot of yelling about that, believe me. But it was too late. She said it had been about her body, her future, so it had been her decision. And part of that decision was to walk away from a relationship where she felt like an afterthought—and to decide against bringing a baby into the situation."

Lexie didn't know how much credence to give to the other woman's thinking. She hadn't known Micah as a marine, but she couldn't picture him as anything except dedicated—probably to the exclusion of all else. She'd seen his ambition for his brewery and knew it was strong. She *had* experienced the consequences of his self-interest of years ago. So she had to allow that the other woman might have had a point about him not making room in his life for anything else. It left Lexie not sure what to say.

Then Micah took a breath, exhaled with a humorless chuckle full of self-disgust and said, "The joke is, I'd been going along thinking I'd made so many strides since you. That I wasn't self-involved anymore…"

Lexie, having eaten enough herself, set her plate on the firepit with his, angling slightly more to face him then. "You hadn't misled her," she pointed out. "This time it was being honest about your plans and what you wanted that caused the problem."

"Yeah, I was riding my high horse thinking that as long as I was clear about what I wanted, what I was working for, I was covered. But I'd missed the second piece of the puzzle—mainly because I *was* so wrapped up in myself. I'd missed that going after what I wanted *without* ever taking anyone else into consideration was as big an issue as not being honest. Adrianna saw it, even if I didn't."

And he seemed to be beating himself up for it.

"I still hadn't learned," he said, "that what my Mom had pushed us to do could translate into just plain selfishness. And because of that, my baby didn't get to be born…"

"A baby you wanted?" Lexie asked softly.

He looked so sad it nearly broke her heart.

"I can't explain it," he said quietly, "but that baby was real to me. And yeah, I wanted it. Once the news sank in, I actually got excited about becoming a dad. Taking that away hit me harder than I ever would have thought it could…"

It wasn't something she would have predicted of him, either. She could hear in his voice that he felt responsible for that baby not being born and was carrying a heavy load of guilt. But once more she wasn't sure what to say.

Treading carefully she chose to say, "Having ambition and focus aren't *bad* things…" She'd often wished Jason had had more of both so he'd want to settle down and build a stable life for them.

"They aren't bad things until you take them to the extreme and they hurt people—like you. They aren't bad things until you can't see beyond them and they cost you your kid," Micah countered.

Lexie wondered if this new realization was a factor in why he was so diligent about helping with the house repairs. But all she said was, "Not getting to become a dad when you discovered that you wanted to was a pricey lesson… I'm sorry."

"Yeah, me, too," he answered. Then, as if he were trying to put a stop to the melancholy atmosphere, he concluded in a lighter vein. "It's just messing with me today."

Lexie wanted to move the subject away from topics that were obviously hurting him, so she smiled and said, "I thought it was my fault so I guess that shows that sometimes none of us can see beyond ourselves."

"Why would you think my lousy mood was your fault?"

Oh. Yeah, that was a reasonable question…

That she didn't want to answer.

Hoping to distract him, she reached for the bakery box, opened it to offer him a cupcake and said, "Chocolate is comfort food…"

He took one out of the box and so did she.

Once it was eaten, Micah gave a rave review of the blend of his stout with the best cupcake he claimed to have ever eaten.

But as glad as she was to hear more enthusiasm in his voice now, it still didn't keep him from going back to that question when they'd finished the cupcakes.

"How could my mood have been your fault?" he reiterated.

Lexie made a face, still hoping to avoid answering.

"Come on—did you do something?" he cajoled. "I'm always the bad guy who has to admit it. If it's your turn, man up," he challenged, relaxing back into the sofa's cushions and stretching an arm along the top edge.

Lexie realized he wasn't going to let her off the hook.

Hating herself for having gotten into this, she sighed before she said, "It was about last night… I shouldn't have…done what I did—"

"Kissed me?" he said, relishing it.

"Yes. And I thought you were stressed out trying to find a way to tell me not to do it again…"

He laughed. Which was a positive change even if she wasn't thrilled that it was at her expense.

Especially since she found herself thinking that he was a man of the world now, while her experience was far more limited. Maybe the kiss that had seemed incredible to her had been barely mediocre to him.

"No, you shouldn't have kissed me," he confirmed when his laughter calmed. "I was close to kissing you and trying to stop myself and you blew that. And then you rocked my world with that kiss and that wasn't fair."

Rocked his world?

So not barely mediocre, after all.

That boosted her confidence.

"*I* rocked your world?" she repeated.

"You were there, right? That was *some* kiss..."

"I thought so..." That had slipped out. "But why wasn't it fair?"

He was serious again but he wasn't brooding any longer, instead he just sounded like he was being sensible. "For me, a kiss like that is the start of something, Lexie," he said. "But for you... What was it?"

"Something I wanted to do and I *couldn't* stop myself..." she confessed.

"It wasn't just you launching yourself out of the marriage gate onto somebody familiar and safe?"

"*Safe?* You? The bad boy of the group? The guy who—"

"Somebody you're safe from any risk of having feelings for," he clarified.

Safe from having feelings for?

That surprised her but it shouldn't have. Until recently she might have said that herself.

But now?

"Actually, *not* being safe from that is on the list of reasons why the kiss was…unwise…" she said softly. "And I wasn't *using* you," she added more firmly since it seemed as if that was part of his concerns, too.

He studied her for a long moment before he said, "So you're *not* safe from having feelings for me?"

She shook her head no but that was as far as she was willing to go.

He went on studying her as if to convince himself that was possible. Then he said, "I guess I had some of my own flashback cautions…"

"I'm not sure what a flashback caution is…"

"The old days make it hard for me to believe that that kiss meant as much to you as it *could* mean to me if I let it…"

"So you didn't let it mean anything to you?" she asked, challenging him this time.

"I've been trying not to…" he answered with a half smile, lifting his hand from the back of the seat to run the side of his index finger along her cheek.

It was so nice that she had to fight the urge to nuzzle into it.

"We do have that history…" he went on quietly. "Plus, you're pretty fresh from being locked into the same guy since we were kids… Seems kind of *unsafe* for me to be on the other side of both of those things…"

"Oooh, so kissing me is dangerous for you… For the big, tough, worldly marine," she joked.

"Sooo dangerous," he said without any levity at all.

Lexie curbed the teasing.

"I don't know what's going on here," she admitted. "And it's strange for me, too. You were one of my best friends. Then you were someone I *hated* for years. Now…you're something else… I keep looking for that shallow, selfish, superficial guy you've been in my head for all these years and instead I just find a guy who isn't any of those things anymore. A guy who's grown up. Who's—"

"Getting to you?" He asked that as if he liked the possibility.

She only conceded to it by raising her eyebrows before she went on. "As for me being fresh out of marriage… I've still been around the block, you know? And my marriage should have broken up a long time ago when I started being unhappy with it. I'm a little ashamed to admit it, but I'm more relieved to have it over with than grieving the end of it…"

She paused, sighed again, then forged on, "The one thing I know for sure is that whatever is happening with you and me doesn't have *anything* to do with the past, and it definitely doesn't have anything to do with Jason."

She wasn't sure why she'd been as candid with Micah as she had been.

Except maybe because it was all true—and his honesty with her about the baby seemed to call for some honesty of her own.

She tried to lighten things again and said, "But if you want to run and hide, I'll understand."

"If I had any sense at all…" he said in a too-sexy voice, his eyes delving deeply into hers.

He stopped stroking her cheek and instead slid his hand to the base of her neck, under hair she'd set free in the car from the bun it had been in all day, bringing her slightly toward him as he leaned in and kissed her.

A kiss that kicked off with an instant bang.

His lips were parted and there was something so innately sensual in them that her own lips had to part, too, had to meet and welcome his tongue when it came.

His hand rose into her hair, cradling her in place as that all-consuming kiss swept her away.

Giving as good as she was getting, she laid her

hands on his pectorals, reveling in that first feel of the muscles she'd been admiring for days.

But rather than soothing her craving, it only whetted her appetite, and when his other arm went around her, pulling her nearer, she took the opportunity to put her arms around him and slide in closer.

The kiss became a plundering of mouths that was arousing feverish things in her. Her back seemed to arch on its own, her breasts yearning for him, for contact with him, straining for it.

And with a mind of their own, too, her hands slipped under his sweatshirt.

Warm and oh-so-sleek over oh-so-many muscles, she reveled in the feel of that solid wall of strength, in the breadth of those shoulders that seemed to go on forever.

But as good as it was to have her hands on his bare skin, it only made her want his hands on hers.

Her front was already plastered against his, her nipples pressed into him, sending their own signal through the thin white blouse she had on. But he didn't seem to be reading the signs.

Or was he still lost in those flashback cautions?

She took a deep breath to expand her chest into his at the same time she opened her mouth a little wider, let her tongue be a little braver and upped the sex quotient of that kiss.

He answered by showing her how it was really

done—almost making her melt—but still he didn't take his hands from those safe spots behind her head and on her back.

Maybe he'd learned some lessons too well...

But he was driving her to distraction, raising a need in her so fierce and overwhelming that she was nearly out of her mind. She started considering physically grabbing his hand and repositioning it on her breast if that was what it took to give him the go-ahead...

A sound rumbled in his throat that made her think he was giving in to something. While the hand on her back stayed in place, the one in her hair took a slow descent down to the outer curve of her breast.

More, more, more!

Lexie inhaled again, expanding into that testing hand on her side.

He appeared to take that as the permission he'd been waiting for, because he brought his hand the rest of the way around to cup her breast. And when she breathed out again it ended up sounding like satisfaction.

But that seemed to unleash him because he stayed only briefly on the outside of her shirt before he had the buttons unfastened and his hand not only deliciously inside her blouse, but under the cups of her bra, too.

And oh, what an adept hand it was...

Big and strong and gentle, he kneaded that tender flesh, circling and tugging and teasing her nipples, turning her to mush, making it impossible for her to think about anything but what he was doing to her.

It was the lower half of her body that went into motion then. One of her jean-clad legs went over his thick thigh and her hips arched in his direction in response to even more hungers coming to life in her.

His hand left her back then to clasp her leg and pull her closer still, not fully on his lap but not far off before giving the same attention to her rump that the other hand was giving to her breasts.

But just when Lexie was pondering tearing off his sweatshirt, he began to slow things down.

He let go of her derriere.

He eased her leg off his.

He repositioned her bra and refastened her blouse even as he cooled off that kiss until it was more sweet than passionate.

And then he stopped even that.

He blew out a long deep breath that somehow sounded as if he were conceding to something really difficult to accept, dropped his forehead to the top of her head and said, "So one of the things I've learned the hard way is that I can't just give in to everything I want when someone else is involved, too…"

He sat up straight. Lexie had the impression that he was shoring up his resolves.

Then he went on, "Right now, what I want is you. In the worst way… And it's not that I don't believe all you said a few minutes ago, but I can't let this go any further until I know you've had time to make sure it's what you want, too. Absolutely, without a doubt, and for no reason other than the fact that you want me as much as I want you…"

"What if I say—"

"Uh-uh," he vetoed before she could say more. "I mean it, Lexie. I have to know that I'm not stacking the deck in any way. That what *I* want is second to what you want."

His hands were loosely around her waist, but he took them away and deflated back against the sofa, putting even more space between them.

"Now do me a favor and go the hell up to bed so I can have a few minutes to pull myself together…"

Lexie tugged at her bottom lip with her teeth, wanting to kiss him again, wanting his hands on her again, wanting him.

But not wanting to ignore what he'd said, because she knew he was right—she *did* need to consider what she was doing.

So she steeled herself against the urges of her body and stood up to go.

Before she could, though, those urges got the

better of her—just a little—and she paused, bent over and kissed the tip of his shoulder.

Then without looking to see if that had even registered with him, she went inside, through the kitchen and upstairs to her room.

All the while wondering how exactly she had come from being friends with Micah and then hating Micah to wanting Micah so much she ached...

Chapter Eight

"Are you afraid he's going to sneak a free cupcake?"

"What?" Lexie asked Jill late on Saturday afternoon.

Lexie and Micah had been together running Micah's booth at the food festival all day. Periodically they'd given each other a break. Lexie was taking one then, sitting on a bench under a tree in Merritt's town square with her friend while Jill's husband was off somewhere else at the festival with the kids.

"You're watching that booth like a hawk," Jill explained. "Or is it Micah you're watching? Last time we talked, you told me you were not a *fan* of Micah Camden and you were sure that nothing would change that. But look at you now, getting an eyeful…"

"I was just watching the booth to see if my cupcakes are selling and if there are more people than he can handle," Lexie claimed.

"Bull," Jill countered, clearly not fooled. "Has he started *handling* you?"

Oh, boy, has he…

And Jill was right, she *had* been staring at Micah. All day long. Every chance she had. She was definitely having trouble taking her eyes off him.

But rather than admit anything she glanced over her shoulder to make sure no one had overheard her friend's lascivious question. "Jill! Shhh…"

"Nobody's listening. But come on, what's going on with you two?"

"We're just working the booth together."

Jill laughed. "Uh-uh. You've joined the fan club," she concluded. "How'd that happen?"

Denial wasn't working so Lexie gave up on it. "I don't know," she said. "But I wouldn't say I'm a *fan*, just that… I don't know… I guess maybe I'm coming to better grips with the past…"

"By *gripping* him?"

"No!" Not that she wasn't thinking about it.

And thinking about it, and thinking about it, and thinking about it…

"It would make such a nice story," her friend suggested. "Childhood best friends hit a rocky road in their teens, go their separate ways, take some hard knocks, then come together again and find true, everlasting love with each other."

"We're just hanging out—admittedly more amicably—and selling beer and cupcakes out of the same booth," Lexie contended.

"Sure you are," Jill said sarcastically. Then, glancing at Micah herself, she said, "Do you like the way he looks better with scruff or without scruff?"

Micah was clean-shaven today—the first time Lexie had seen him that way since she'd been back. It had been a surprise this morning and yes, that had been part of her study of him as the day had gone on—trying to decide which look she preferred.

"I don't think it matters," she said, giving her final verdict. He was hella-handsome with and without—more rugged-looking with, more businesslike without, but equally as hot either way. "He did it so he'd look more professional," she explained, sharing the reason he'd given to her.

"Did you watch?"

"Watch him shave? No!" Although it was an interesting idea that Lexie hadn't thought of before.

"I like to watch Anthony shave," Jill said. "It always gets me going."

Lexie laughed and shook her head at her friend's outrageousness.

"How about you," Jill asked then. "Did you like to watch Jason shave?"

"No," Lexie said honestly. "He always had that smooth baby face, you know? His beard never came in in more than thin patches and even if he missed a day, you could feel it but you couldn't really see it."

But thinking about that, about her ex, Lexie thought about how little sex appeal he'd actually had in comparison to Micah—Micah, who seemed to exude it from every pore.

Jason's build had stayed boyish, skinny even. His biceps hadn't looked much different than Lexie's.

But still she'd found him appealing because she'd loved him.

Now, with Micah, the physical attraction was monumental, but her feelings were more confusing.

"With Anthony, what came first for you?" she asked her friend. "Sex or love?"

Jill laughed again. "Sex," she said without hesitation. "Are you kidding? He's a big, brawny, beautiful fireman."

"You didn't have any feelings for him before you went to bed with him?"

"I did. I think I was on the brink of loving him and sex was what pushed it over the edge. Why? Are you thinking about sleeping with Micah?" Jill's voice was full of delight and titillation. Until, with shock, she said, "Or are you thinking you might be falling for him? Because that's more than just being a fan..."

"There's just a lot of stuff going on..."

"*Have* you slept together?"

"No."

"But you want to!" her friend said, sounding absolutely certain.

Lexie didn't answer that. But she was staring at Micah again because no, she couldn't take her eyes off him.

Not only was he clean-shaven today, but he had on dress slacks and a crisp pale blue shirt with the sleeves rolled to his elbows. The dressier style smoothed some of his edges and gave him a dashing look that was irresistible.

And yes, she did want to finish what they'd started the night before.

She just didn't know if she should...

"Want my two cents' worth?" Jill said.

Lexie laughed. "Like I could stop you."

"If you even *think* you might be falling for him and if you're even *entertaining* the idea of sleeping with him, you have *got* to do it, Lex."

Lexie laughed at her friend's forceful declaration. "Not a question in your mind, huh?"

"And if Micah wants to, too, that makes three reasons why you'd better do it."

"How do you figure?"

"It's the only way to give you both the whole *present-day* picture and a reality check," Jill decreed authoritatively.

"Still not sure what you're getting at," Lexie said.

"I'd say look at him, but you're already doing that," her friend began, "but first of all, he's just one great big tower of sexy, gorgeous guy now. So it's no wonder he's got you all churned up. You have to get that out of your system before you can know how much simple attraction might be coloring things for you. And only when you've done that will you be able to judge what it is you're really feeling for him—are you genuinely falling for him or do you just need some close-order drill with him. That's what solved it for me with Anthony— I just wanted him so much I couldn't be sure if it was because he was such a hunk or because he was such a hunk *and* I loved him."

"Okay, that's one," Lexie said, seeing some sense in that.

"Two, it isn't only your current feelings that could be clouded by the churned-up thing," Jill contended. "There's senior year and what Micah did, too. The only way you're going to be able to judge if you've really forgiven him for that or if the churned-up thing has just thrown a tarp over it, is to get the churned-up thing calmed down. Once it is, the tarp will get pulled away and you'll see if you still resent Micah underneath it."

Also reasonable.

"And three?"

"There's Micah's side. His feelings for you when we were kids had to have been *extreme* for him to do what he did. There could be some flicker of that old flame and he could be carrying around a teenage fantasy of what finally having you would be like. You want—and need—that worked out of *his* system so he's only left with present-day reality, too."

Also reasonable.

But none of it romantic.

"You definitely know how to make a clinical case for doing it," Lexie said.

And how to cool her off in the process.

"I'm just saying there's a lot to sift through between the two of you and I think sex might be the tool for the job."

"Still clinical, Jill," Lexie judged.

But she had to admit that her friend had made some decent points.

And had given her more to think about…

* * *

"Oh! Hey…"

When Micah appeared from inside the house at the back door late Saturday night, Lexie was sitting where they'd had dinner the night before—on the curved wicker sofa at the fire pit.

"Hi," she returned. "I heard fireworks going off when I got out of the shower," she said, pointing at the sky to explain what she was doing out there.

"Yesterday was the last day of school for seniors around here. I heard the Cartwright twins had a big party planned—fireworks included," Micah informed.

"They're putting on a good show. Come watch."

"I'll be right there," he promised, disappearing in the direction of the sunroom.

The food festival had gone on until ten o'clock. They'd both needed to arrive separately in the morning and also had to go their own ways when it was over—Micah loading kegs and equipment into his truck to return to the brewery, Lexie needing to take borrowed display towers, trays and racks back to the bakery and wash them before she could drive home in her own car.

It had been a long day and with Micah still in the brewery when she got home, Lexie had headed upstairs to take the shower she had been dying for after so many hours outdoors.

She could have just gotten into bed when she'd

finished that but instead she'd blow-dried her hair, applied a hint of color to her cheekbones and a thin line of eyeliner to her lids.

Then, rather than putting on pajamas, she'd opted for something between those and street clothes—a lounging set made up of a charcoal colored V-neck T-shirt over a pair of lighter gray shorts—both of them loose-fitting and not at all sexy.

It was the lace demi-cup bra and matching bikinis underneath that provided the sex appeal. Just in case…

And it *was* just in case because after spending the entire day with Micah, there was no indication that last night had ever happened. There hadn't been a single mention of anything. There hadn't been any meaningful glances. Any fleeting touches or brushes against each other. There hadn't even been any bantering between them.

And not just because there were other people around. Even in the lulls between customers when they'd been alone, things had been purely cool and detached. If anything, Micah had deliberately busied himself as far away from her as he could get.

Things had been so impersonal that she'd begun to wonder if *he'd* thought about last night with a cooler head and talked himself out of taking it any further.

So a very casual, very loose T-shirt and shorts made up her outfit of choice.

With some underwear that could be a potential surprise or remain her secret forever.

Besides, what Jill had said *had* cooled *her* off some.

The idea that Micah could be working out an old fantasy was haunting her. Especially if that meant the fantasy might be put to rest for him once and for all as soon as it was fulfilled.

So all the way around she thought it was better to be cautious tonight.

Micah was gone only a few minutes before he reappeared at the back door and came outside to join her.

Sneaking a peek at him from the corner of her eyes, Lexie saw that his hair was shower damp, and he'd shaved again so his face was still completely clear of scruff.

He wasn't in pajamas, either—instead, wearing his well-worn jeans and yet another navy blue crewneck T-shirt with the Marine insignia. Unlike what Lexie had changed into, though, his T-shirt fitted him like a second skin and nearly made her mouth water.

Which was why she determinedly directed her view back to the fireworks.

Only comments about those fireworks passed between them until the lights in the sky ended in several overlapping bursts, and the far-off sound of clapping and whistling came from the neighboring farm.

"That was a nice end to today," Micah noted, angling toward Lexie and again laying one arm across the top of the sofa's back.

"So," Micah said then. "We emptied every keg, sold every case of beer and every cupcake, and still had folks wanting more when we were closing up at the end. I'd say that means we did pretty well today."

"I think we did great," Lexie chimed in.

"Did it convince you to buy the bakery?"

"I was pretty convinced before, but it definitely helped—along with all the enthusiasm for my baking… I forgot how news travels here. I didn't think anyone knew and instead everyone did."

"Small towns," Micah said. "But having everyone hoping you *do* buy the bakery is better than having everyone telling you not to."

"True. I think I'll talk to Nessa on Monday about the financing. Either way, after working there yesterday, and today's festival, I'm sure it's what I want to do."

"Good for you!"

"And today was good for you," she pointed out. "You even got interviewed by a network news crew!"

"The marketing people for Camden Superstores

arranged that. It was the first in a bunch of things they have set up to get the word out for the launch of the stouts in the stores."

"Are you going to be ready for that soon?"

He let out a worried sounding laugh. "I hope so. We're working hard to be."

"But you're still experimenting with the flavored stouts. And we never got to the tasting you wanted me to do last night."

"That's okay. The first launch is just for the plain ones, anyway. The flavored ones will be a second wave so they can get highlighted on their own. And you can do the tasting tomorrow." He raised the index finger that was near her shoulder and tapped her. "That reporter loved your cupcakes, too," he reminded.

"She bought a whole dozen," Lexie said, having been pleased by that. The food festival had been one big reunion, bringing out a constant stream of familiar faces. And while Lexie hoped those familiar faces had purchased the cupcakes because they wanted to, and given compliments they meant, it was a little hard to know for sure. Friends and acquaintances of hers, of Micah's, of her parents', of Gertie's might have just been buying and complimenting out of kindness. But she could rely on the opinion of a network news reporter who was a complete stranger.

"And her photographer bought another dozen, didn't he?" Micah added.

"Along with *two* cases of beer," Lexie pointed out.

Micah's grin showed how happy that had made him. "I think we both did okay," he concluded.

Since he seemed ready for a change of subject Lexie nodded at his clean-shaven face and then at his chest stretching the knit of his T-shirt. "And then there was you... No beard and all dressed up in clothes that weren't military issue?"

His grin this time showed some humility. "I told you I shaved so I'd look more businesslike. And I sank every penny I have into the brewery when I got out of the Marines. I couldn't spare much for civvies so my closet is all military issue until I'm making some money. Those pants and that shirt were an investment for me."

"Well, it payed off—you looked great all business-manned-up."

His eyes dropped for a mere second to what she was wearing and he said somewhat under his breath, "And you look great right now..."

"Did I look bad all day?" she asked in mock offense.

"No, you looked good then, too. And every other day..."

So maybe he was starting things again?

If he was, Lexie wasn't sure she was ready for

it. Instead, she said, "So your plain stouts are ready to go, your flavored stouts aren't far behind, your brewery is up and running and now you've had your soft launch with publicity already started for the formal launch... You're on your way. What does your life look like in five years?"

He laughed wryly. "I haven't thought much beyond any of that."

But he looked off into the distance and seemed to give some thought to it now in order to answer her question.

After a moment, he said, "I'm in Merritt to stay. I like the brewery being out Gertie's back door and having her input, so as long as she'll have me and I can meet the demands of the superstores with this setup, I'd like to stay here."

He paused and seemed to be thinking more before he went on. "And I want to get married, have a family, build the kind of life I've seen people around here have."

After seeing his sorrow over almost becoming a father, that made sense. Plus, now that he'd left the Marines and had his life's goal underway, he was at that point in his timetable that allowed for it.

He looked back at her then. "What about you? What's your five-year plan?"

She laughed. "I have the plan for next week that I told you about—right now I'm just proud of that!"

He smiled but didn't push her for more. Instead,

he changed the subject again. "I couldn't believe Gertie came out today."

"With poor Mary pushing that wheelchair! I don't know if that was a good idea. I was glad when you offered to push it back to the apartment."

"After Mary had made the rounds to all the other booths and scored enough samples and tasters for two days," he said with another laugh. "Gertie said on the way back that they thought the wheelchair was actually going to be a help, making it easier to transport things home so they could really load up."

"I told them when I was there this morning before the festival started that I'd bring them whatever they wanted."

"They were afraid the elk chili would all be gone before you could score some. And they also wanted to get out and have a little while at the festival," Micah said.

"Against doctor's orders."

"Gertie didn't seem the worse for wear when I got her back."

Lexie could confirm that that was true because she had spent one of her early evening breaks at the apartment.

"Nobody's gonna keep her down, not even you," Micah warned.

"Or broken bones," Lexie said wryly.

"You gotta love her," was Micah's amused comment on that.

"I do. I just worry about her, too."

He nodded his understanding. "And how's Jill? The two of you were deep into talking about something…"

You…

Lexie decided to tell him, wanting to gauge his reaction. "She's wondering about you and me… wondering if you're playing out a teenage fantasy…"

He made an unpleasant face. "That's a revolting idea. And just FYI—the fantasies I'm having about you now are all brand spanking new." Then he seemed to think twice and said, "Is that why you're giving me a little of the cold shoulder tonight?"

"I'm not," she protested.

"A little," he persisted.

Because she hadn't flirted back with him a few minutes earlier? Or *had* something changed in her behavior toward him?

"You know," Micah said then, "puberty hormones are a funny thing. For me, they cropped up, aimed in one direction—at you—and after that… Will it piss you off if I say after that nothing mattered, not even you as a person?"

"Are you saying that I became a piece of meat to you?"

"That sounds bad! And no, that's not exactly what I'm saying. I'm saying that you became something I just *had* to have and it wouldn't have mattered if you robbed banks or kicked dogs or took candy from babies because it was an obsession. Like those weird red boots you wanted when we were sophomores—remember those?"

Lexie grimaced. "They were so horrible!"

"No argument here," he agreed. "They were some kind of cross between a cowboy boot and a combat boot—shiny red leather, pointy steal-tipped toes, studs up the sides, those soles—"

"Patent leather platforms," she named them for him.

"I always thought they should have come with a whip," he said, laughing.

Lexie made another face.

"But nothing any of us said about them changed your mind—you *had* to have them. You worked yourself to the bone flipping burgers, you nearly flunked biology because you were working too many hours to get homework done or study for tests. You spent a *fortune* on those damn things…"

All true. And yes, she remembered her obsession with them.

"You told us more than once how you saw yourself in those boots, walking down the halls of school in them—your Power Boots, you called them… You had some kind of fantasy about those boots, about yourself when you wore them, didn't you?"

She had, but she only acknowledged it with a raise of her chin.

"That was a teenage obsession, right?"

Another raise of her chin.

"And now? Are any of those fantasies about those red boots still alive and thriving in you?"

She didn't even like remembering those awful boots. "No," she admitted.

"So why would any fantasies I had then be any more long-lived than that? Believe me, I didn't set eyes on you at the airport and think, *Maybe now's my chance*," he said facetiously. "At first, when you got back to Merritt, you were just a bad page out of my past. If not for Gertie and what had happened here with the damage to the houses, I would have given you a wide berth."

Lexie recalled that he'd been more patient and friendly toward her than she'd been toward him at the start but she had to admit that there hadn't been anything that made her think he was angling for a second chance.

"Things just...*developed* from there," he went on. "You're different than who you were growing up, too. We're both whole human beings now—"

"As opposed to?"

"As opposed to two teenagers who were still

figuring themselves out. What's on my mind about you now has nothing to do with anything then."

"What *is* on your mind about me now?"

His smile was lopsided and sweet. "What I liked about you when we were kids is still there—your sense of humor, your boldness, that you never shrink from giving me a hard time. But now, I also see that you've suffered your own wounds and risen out of them. That you know your own mind. That you've circled back around to find a new place in Merritt the same way I have. That the things that are important to me are important to you, too."

She hadn't expected such a long list.

Then he paused, a flicker of wickedness coming into his eyes as he added. "And you're so damn beautiful I can't get enough of looking at you, and my hands are literally itching to run all over that body..."

And yet rather than reach for her he actually leaned slightly farther back, putting a few inches of distance from where his hand had been near enough to her shoulder to tap it earlier.

Then, without any guile or flirtation or insinuation at all, he said, "But..."

"But?" Lexie prompted when he didn't elaborate.

"Everything I said at the end of last night stands."

She knew what he meant. Last night he'd said

he wouldn't go any further until she was certain that it was what she wanted, too. And unless she convinced him of that, she knew he wouldn't make another move.

Since talking to Jill, she *had* thought more clearly. But as she took a long look at him, she went over it in her mind again just to be sure.

She thought about his first response to the suggestion that he might be acting on some long-ago fantasies—that it was *revolting*—and realized that that response had had the ring of truth to it.

She thought about those horrible red boots of hers, how much they'd dominated her image of herself and how far she'd come from what had definitely been a teenage obsession.

She thought about the fact that she was no longer the girl who young Micah had had a crush on—the girl who had been more outlandish, more outrageous just for the sake of getting noticed, of showing off.

None of that was a part of her now and she had to think that that teenage bravado in her had likely had a role in what the push-the-limits Micah had found appealing.

Of course, she couldn't know without a doubt what was in Micah's mind. She could only trust him—and herself. And when she analyzed what her instincts were telling her, she had her answer.

"What *were* your teenage fantasies about me?" she asked, letting a hint of flirtation seep into her tone.

He raised an eyebrow at her as if asking if she really wanted to know that. When she held her ground he said, "Actually they were almost more about me than you—I was pure ego then, you know? They were about me being your hero, rushing in to save you from peril, and you not being able to resist me from that minute on. Me strolling in in a new jacket that made me look like a tough guy and you getting turned on because I had so much more edge than nice-guy Jason..." He smiled at what he seemed to be recalling. "Me beating up some jerk for making fun of you in those red boots, you trading up to the stud who could take down guys like that for you. That kind of thing."

Lexie doubted those examples covered everything but she only said, "I think the red boots are still in Gram's attic—you want me to put them on, see if we can get someone to make fun of me so you can beat them up?"

He made two fists. "These are lethal weapons—I'd end up in jail," he joked.

But looking at the size of those fists, Lexie thought they probably could be lethal weapons.

And still all she really wanted was to have his hands doing more of what they'd done the night before. She snaked her fingers into his fists, between his fingers, and pressed her palms to his.

"Before I talked to Jill, I still wasn't thinking with a cool head," Lexie confessed quietly.

"But after?" he asked, tightening his grip on her hands.

"A whole lot cooler."

He nodded in a reserved way that told her that if she was telling him no, he would accept it.

"How about you?" she asked then. "Your head seemed pretty cool all day."

"Don't be fooled—things are still sizzling inside of me."

"That sounds painful," she joked with a smile she hoped was as wicked as his had been a moment earlier. Wicked and alluring…

"If you're not feeling the pain, too, I'm not budging," he challenged.

Knowing what she was starting here sent a shiver of anticipation through her. "I wouldn't call it pain exactly…" she mused. "But I do need something done about it…"

"Is that so?" he said with a deep chuckle.

"Any ideas?"

"A few," he tempted, using their entangled hands to pull her toward him.

Lexie thought he'd done it to kiss her but instead, with her face close to his, he looked intently into her eyes.

He must have been reassured by what he saw because his own eyelids lowered to half-mast and the smile that came along was happy and full of the promise of delight.

Then his supple lips parted, his head tilted and he kissed her. Chastely, tentatively, invitingly, but as if he were giving her the opportunity to still step away.

Which Lexie had no intention of doing.

She proved that by escalating their kiss, sending her tongue to do a little audacious flirting of its own.

She felt him smile at that. He let go of her hands and cupped both sides of her face as the kiss became open-mouthed and very, very steamy.

Her hands dropped to his thighs where she felt the massive muscles she'd only ogled in the past, working them just a little and thinking about that other part of him not so much farther up, raising her own desire another notch.

They went on kissing, mouths opening wider, tongues going from cat-and-mouse to thrust-and-parry. But hands stayed where they were, even though Lexie's need to feel those hands of his everywhere else grew and grew.

Micah ended the kiss and looked into her eyes again.

"You're sure about this?" he asked in a gravelly voice.

"I am. Are you?"

He laughed. "Yeah, pretty sure..." he understated, taking one of her hands in his and pulling her with him off the sofa.

"Upstairs or down?" he said.

"Upstairs but… I don't have any…"

"I put a few in my pocket earlier."

A few?

Oh…

"Then upstairs," she said with some laughter in her voice.

That's where he took her, leading her into her bedroom with moonlight's glow to brighten the space with a milky illumination.

It was enough to glisten off his dark hair and highlight that sculpted face when he spun her around into another kiss—this one sensual enough to keep her mouth captive and his hands free.

Hers went to his chest and his clamped around her upper arms, giving a massage similar to what she'd done to his thighs.

Then it was her shoulders he cupped and squeezed, her shoulder blades, lower on her back, lower still to her derriere…

His big hands were doing such wonderful things but as good as they felt right where they were, she wished he were doing those same things to breasts that were straining for him.

But in the meantime, she decided to satisfy another hunger and slipped her hands under his T-shirt to again lay her palms to his sleek skin, this time caressing the pectorals that had fed her own fantasies.

The problem with those tightly fitting T-shirts was that they were too constrictive and Lexie wanted him freed from that particular one.

So she raised her hands up to his broad shoulders, taking the shirt with them—breaking away from that kiss to pull it over his head.

She kissed him again, but not on the mouth. Instead, she pressed her lips to one of those pectorals before she veered back just enough to finally see his bare chest.

His oh-so-grand bare chest...

Micah used that opportunity to reach for the hem of her T-shirt and roll it upward, taking it off to drop to the floor with his.

With that gone, his hands came to her sides, the heels of them just barely riding the outer swells of her breasts. But tonight, it wasn't about needing encouragement. Instead, it was as if he were savoring every step, every moment on the way to the next.

And in the next moment, both of his hands cupped her breasts.

She wished she'd gone braless. Even the demi-cups felt like too much in the way of nipples that were screaming for the feel of his palms, for his fingers working her pliable flesh.

Then he abandoned her breasts altogether to unhook her bra and she got her wish.

Leaving one hand splayed against her back, his other returned to her breasts until her knees were weak.

He stopped then, scooped her up and laid her on the bed, leaning over to kiss her again while he slipped her shorts off and unfastened his jeans.

But he didn't remove them and Lexie wasn't letting *that* go on. She sat up enough to grasp his waistband.

Micah stopped her long enough to take protection from his jeans pocket and toss the packets on the bed before he let her dispose of the only thing he was wearing on the bottom.

Lexie couldn't help laughing to herself at the thought that he'd come prepared with a surprise of his own. Then she put an end to that kiss and fell back, allowing herself the opportunity to look at him in all his glory. To see if he was as magnificent everywhere as she'd imagined him to be.

There was no disappointment. He was even better than she'd guessed and that sight of him took her desire for him up to an entirely new level.

He removed her bikini panties, too, and indulged in just enough of a look at her naked body to bring a smile to his handsome face before he joined her on the bed and pure, primitive need was let loose.

His mouth found hers again and then deserted it for a breast that he engulfed in wet warmth while his hand kept the other one engaged.

Tugging at her nipple with careful teeth, flicking the tip with a pointed tongue, teasing and tormenting her. She tried to keep from writhing but couldn't.

Especially not when his other hand began to travel.

There was something extraordinary about how he touched her and kissed her, about everything he did—even in the muscular thigh that curved over one of hers and nestled up into the V of her legs.

Inhibition was gone but everything he did was slow and tender and alert to even the slightest response so he knew just how hard or soft, how long or short, how rough or how gentle to make every caress to maximize her enjoyment.

He wasn't lost in himself and his gratification, and instead was so in tune with her that he seemed to know what she wanted, what she needed, almost before she did. That was a first for her. A first that made everything so much more intense. So much better...

Not wanting to be the only one of them in the throes of such pleasure, though, she explored his body, reveling in all that smooth-silk-over-steel musculature before she reached for the long hard proof that he was as worked up about her as she was about him. She stroked him, hoping to drive him wild, too.

And if the guttural moan that rumbled in his throat was any indication, she succeeded.

His hand glided it down her stomach then and his knee freed the way for it to slip between her legs in its place. Her spine arched in reflex and her grip around him tightened just enough to elicit a flex in him as one finger found a path inside her.

The intensity of it stole her breath for a moment and made her writhe a little more with all he was arousing.

But as she approached a near frenzy of wanting him, he rolled over to find one of the condoms he'd thrown onto the mattress and use it. When he rolled back, he spread her thighs with his knee and repositioned himself between them, slipping something so much more substantial than his fingers into her instead.

A soft moan echoed in her throat as her hips angled upward into his. She clamped around him to hold him there in order to prolong how amazing it felt.

But there was only a momentary pause before the strength of his hips pulled out of that hold. Just far enough, just briefly enough to build her anticipation, only to delve back in even deeper.

Out again and then in deeper still, in and out,

every retreat, every return increasing the urgency in her.

Faster, harder, speed grew and Lexie kept up, clinging to his back, matching him until their bodies raced together to a peak that exploded in her like nothing she'd ever known, robbing her of every thought and leaving her held in exquisite suspension from time or place, where nothing existed but Micah and what he'd awakened in her.

Just as that started to decline, his climax hit. When he plunged all the way into her in his own explosion, she curled her legs around him to bring him as far into the core of her as he could go. At that moment, something that hadn't ever happened before struck her and she was carried away to a second pinnacle even better, stronger, longer lasting than the first.

A second pinnacle that—when it began to ebb—left her drained just as Micah's big body was settling atop hers.

For a while, neither of them moved, replete and speechless in the aftermath.

Then Lexie heard herself say in nothing more than a faint whisper of revelation, "Oh…"

"What? Did I hurt you?" Micah asked in alarm, raising to his forearms and lifting some of his weight off her.

"No," she assured him in a hurry, "I just didn't

know it could be like that…" Because it never had been before.

In response, he gave her a profound, meaningful kiss. Then he slid out of her, got off the bed and disappeared into her bathroom.

When he came back, he lay beside her, insinuated an arm underneath her back and brought her close to his side.

"Don't scare me like that," he said as if there hadn't been an interruption. "I thought I did something wrong."

Lexie could only laugh at that notion. "Mmm… according to the textbook *I* read, you did everything right. Really, really, *really* right…"

"Does that mean I get to do it again?"

Oh, definitely… she thought, hoping that his enthusiasm meant that her one-partner training hadn't disappointed him.

But what she said was a saucy, "Maybe. If you give me a minute to regroup."

"I'll need a little more than a minute but…not too much more," he answered tantalizingly.

His arm tightened around her while the rest of him relaxed, and her own body sank against his side, fused so perfectly there that it was as if she'd found her match.

That was also something new. Something unique. And so was the sense that she'd somehow landed exactly where she was supposed to be…

But even as that thought went through her mind exhaustion overcame her and she had to surrender to it.

Chapter Nine

"Where would Lexie have gone so early in the morning?"

Gertie's question was a good one. Micah had asked it himself, too—about a hundred times since waking up. Since waking up alone in Lexie's bed to the sound of her cell phone ringing on her nightstand after a night full of lovemaking and falling asleep with her beautiful body tucked safely in his arms.

Ordinarily, he was a light sleeper. But after the fourth time they'd made love, he'd conked out so soundly that somewhere between then—around 5:00 a.m.—and eight o'clock when Gertie had called, Lexie had slipped out of his arms, out of bed and out of the house without him having any inkling.

"And then there's you," Gertie said as if she was doggedly on the trail of a solution to a mystery. "Your stouts had their maiden voyage at the food festival and were a big hit. Your brewery is on its way. But instead of riding high today, you look like hell. I haven't seen you this down in the mouth since everything hit the fan when you were in high school."

Micah studied the television's remote control as if it held the solution to all the world's problems and didn't respond to the elderly woman's rant.

Gertie went on, anyway. "I thought you and Lexie were friends again. She's been so happy to be helping out with the flavored stouts until I can do it. She gives you credit for the bakery idea—it's all sounded good and it looked like you were getting along just fine yesterday. Did you have a fight or something last night?"

"No, we didn't have a fight." *Not in the slightest.* "We've been doing great." *Sooo great...*

Last night had been like no night, no day, no time he'd ever had with any woman anywhere. So great he'd never wanted it to end. So great he'd fallen asleep thinking he'd do anything to make it last.

Only to wake up and find Lexie gone.

But he was trying to keep Gertie from knowing he'd slept with her granddaughter so he said, "Maybe she went for a walk—"

"It's ten o'clock and you said she wasn't back when you left—she could have walked to Kansas by now!"

"Maybe she went to have breakfast with Jill. Maybe she needed to do something at the bakery—she used all of Nessa's stuff for her cupcakes, maybe she had cleanup she needed to go back to do—"

"Did she take the car or the truck?"

"I didn't notice," Micah lied. He knew Lexie had taken Gertie's sedan but he didn't want Gertie to realize he'd been paying attention to that. "Whatever she left to do, she just forgot her phone," he concluded. "I was in the kitchen when you called, I hollered for her but there was no answer, and I was afraid something might have happened with you, so I picked up…"

All but the locations of that account of events were true. Then, when he'd found out what Gertie needed and hung up, he'd searched everywhere for Lexie until he'd had to admit that she'd bolted.

"You didn't have to be so Johnny-on-the-spot for this. It wasn't that important," Gertie was saying. "We just needed somebody to fix our TV so it wouldn't be in Spanish—neither one of us could figure out how we did that…"

"I didn't want you sitting here alone, watching TV in Spanish while Mary went to church," Micah said just as he resolved the issue. Besides, once he'd known Lexie was nowhere to be found, he hadn't been able to calm down enough to sit still, so he had decided he might as well do what he could for Gertie.

"I don't like that Lexie doesn't at least have her phone," Gertie said, starting up again.

"Like I said, I'm sure she just forgot it and I'm also sure she's fine."

"I don't think you're sure about anything," the elderly woman said. "I think the two of you got into it and you don't want to admit it."

Got into it meaning that they'd fought, not the way they really *had* gotten into it, Micah thought.

"We didn't fight, Gert," he repeated honestly.

And apparently something about the way he said it tweaked something in Gertie because her eyes got very big before she said, "Ohhh…" as if light was dawning on something interesting and scandalous.

He thought he'd better get out of there before this got any worse.

"Your TV is fixed so I'm gonna take off. Unless you need me to do something else." He set the remote on the TV tray beside Gertie's wheelchair.

Her shock seemed to have passed because she was sitting there with a Cheshire cat grin on her lined face. "The two of you are *more* than friends," she deduced.

I guess not if Lexie ran out this morning...

"Is my granddaughter home in bed and you're letting her sleep off a big night?" the elderly woman said.

I wish...

The fallout he was suffering from Lexie leaving him high and dry must have shown on his face because Gertie sobered instantly with another far more ominous, "Ohhh..." Followed by, "Did she have morning-after remorse and run out on you?"

"Jeez, Gertie!"

But Lexie had definitely run out on him and morning-after remorse was exactly what he was worried about.

Along with the fear that the night they'd spent together hadn't meant to her what it had to him.

Along with wondering why the hell it *had* meant so much to him.

Along with so many whys...

"I don't know what's going on, Gert," he said then. "I don't know what's going on with Lexie. I don't know what's going on with me—"

"So something *is* going on between the two of you!"

"Gertie, you have to leave this alone. Please... We did *not* have a fight and whatever is going on we'll have to work out."

Unless they couldn't…

But he didn't want to think about that. He *couldn't* think about that.

"Patience, Micah," Gertie advised then. "With beer and with Lexie…"

Because the ink was barely dry on her divorce papers. He'd been kicking himself all morning, thinking that maybe he should have bided his time. That maybe he *had* just been a rebound for her, a testing of her wings, a practice run to get her feet wet.

But then he was also remembering what he'd done that had hurt her when they were teenagers, what he'd done that had caused so much damage that she'd hated him for over a decade, and worrying that something about that had resurfaced and that she might not be able to forgive him for it.

And if that wasn't enough, he was remembering as well that she'd been fretting over the idea that he wanted her as a way of acting on that old crush—which had him wondering if he'd done something to make her think that last night *had* been about that.

He was just in a bad spiral, a bad headspace, and he didn't know what to do about it…

"I gotta go, Gert," he said. "I really do…"

He went to the apartment door.

"Micah!" Gertie said with the bark of a drill sergeant.

He stopped with his hand on the knob and looked over his shoulder at the woman he considered his friend and mentor, the woman he considered family.

"It'll work out," she said in a softer, more comforting voice.

He could only answer with a raise of his chin that pretended to believe her.

"When I see her, I'll tell her to call you," he promised.

"I know," the elderly woman said with the kind of confidence she'd always shown in him, even when he hadn't deserved it.

Appreciating that as much now as he had then, he left the apartment and got in his truck. But he didn't start the engine, he just sat there, looking around for any sign of Lexie, of the car she'd taken.

He didn't find a single one.

He thought about going to Jill's house. He thought about driving up and down every street of Merritt. He thought about going anywhere Lexie might have gone—about every pond, every lake, every field, every barn, every hangout they'd frequented as kids that she might revisit for who-knew-what reason.

And again he thought why, why, why hadn't she just stayed in bed with him...

Then Gertie's advice to have patience echoed in his mind and he decided not to do anything but go back to the house, hoping she might be there now, deciding to wait there for her if she wasn't. Regardless of how hard it would be for him to do that.

He turned the key in the ignition and pulled out of the parking spot, thinking that this was *not* how he'd pictured this morning when he'd fallen asleep a few hours ago.

But how could he have guessed this would happen after the night they'd had? When Lexie had been as into everything as he'd been? When she'd enjoyed it as much as he had—enough to instigate that fourth time herself. How could he have guessed this would happen when she'd curled up against him afterward as if it were where she'd been sleeping forever?

He *couldn't* have guessed this would happen— and he certainly *wouldn't* have guessed it when he'd been thinking that having her curled up against him was where he *wanted* her to sleep.

Every night from last night on…

No, this wasn't a twist he'd seen coming.

And it was like taking a battering ram to the gut…

"Okay, pull it together," he ordered himself as he turned onto the road that led out of town and toward the Parker farm.

It took him a few miles, a few deep breaths, a few reminders that he was a marine trained to handle anything, before he gained any kind of control over himself.

But when he'd managed that, it helped.

And he started to sort through his own thoughts. And feelings.

He hadn't been lying when he'd told Lexie that his old crush was long gone, long dead. It was.

But in its place was something else, he realized now. Something new. Something that had started the way the crush had but had become so much more.

He'd been determined *not* to flip that switch, not to let his feelings become more, become something potent and deep-rooted.

The trouble was he hadn't been able to keep that switch from flipping.

And now that it had, he knew that those feelings for her were *not* a schoolboy crush.

They weren't centered around him or his ego, they weren't superficial or fleeting.

They were definitely deep-rooted, they were intense, they were unshakable.

And they were very, very real.

"Oh, my God, Gertie, I'm in love with her…"

He pulled over to the side of the country road he was on and stared into space, lost in that recognition that rippled through him.

He was in love with someone who could have woken up this morning hating his guts again.

He was in love with someone who he suddenly knew without a doubt he wanted to spend the rest of his life with, who might want to never set eyes on him again…

Was this the universe doling out the ultimate punishment to him?

"It'd be a good one," he said. Because what could hurt him more?

He stayed there on the side of that road for a long time, torturing himself by mentally exploring what he now knew he wanted—in the same moment, he was sure he'd never have it…

First and foremost, he wanted Lexie. And not like he'd wanted her as a kid—not as a trophy, not as a victory over a competitor, not as the answer to his own self-centered fantasies.

He wanted her as his wife. The person he could build a life with, raise a family with.

He wanted her as his sounding board, his advisor—because even though their businesses were separate, they still made a good team when it came to hashing out problems, brainstorming, helping each other.

He wanted to always have that feeling he had every time she walked into a room—that feeling that there wasn't light or warmth until she was there with him.

He wanted to always have her hand to hold.

He wanted to always have her by his side to face whatever life threw at them.

And there was a really good chance that he

might never have any of that because, once again, he might be the only one of them to feel this way…

"Oh, Gertie, what the hell am I gonna do?" he whispered.

But as much as the drive to do something—*anything*—urged him to pull out all the stops, to go to any lengths, to hatch plots and ploys and strategies to get Lexie to be his, he sighed a deep sigh and resigned himself to doing nothing. To having that patience Gertie had told him to have. To hoping—and God help him, praying—for the best.

And to accepting her decision, whatever it might be—even if she decided she didn't want those same things with him.

There was that battering ram to the gut again…

Because never had he reached a harder decision.

But one way or another he was determined that, should he need to, he would see it through.

And that if Lexie hated him again, if Lexie didn't have the same kind of feelings for him that he had for her, if he could never have her, that's the way it would have to be.

He just didn't know how he would survive it…

Going home to face Micah was not easy.

Lexie had hoped that he might still be asleep, that he might not know she'd ever left. She'd hoped that she could sneak in the way she'd sneaked out, play it cool and that he'd never know the difference.

Instead, when she pulled up in front of her grandmother's farmhouse, he was standing on the front porch, leaning one wide shoulder against the porch post.

He was dressed again in camo pants, combat boots and a tan Marine-issue T-shirt, his biceps stretching the short sleeves taut, his muscular forearms crossed over his flat stomach. His striking face was once more stubbled with dark beard and he couldn't have looked more somber as he watched her approach. And still, to her, just that initial sight of him fed a craving in her.

"Hi," he greeted her, his tone full of questions.

"Hi," Lexie responded with some guilt in hers.

"Are you okay?"

It was nice that her well-being was the first thing he addressed. He didn't even sound angry, despite the fact that she'd so stealthily gathered jeans, a T-shirt and a pair of flip-flops to sneak out of the room like a thief in the night. She'd dressed downstairs and slipped away without leaving him any explanation. And after all their hours together before that, he'd earned better treatment.

"I'm okay…" she said without much certainty.

As she climbed the stairs to join him on the porch, he pivoted out of her way, his stance the same, just facing her rather than looking out at the road she'd driven in on.

"I just…uh…freaked out," she confessed when he left it up to her to make the next move.

"Okay," he said as if he were bracing himself. "You had regrets—"

"Regrets? No!" She'd been so lost in her own issues that it hadn't occurred to her that he might have thought she was sorry for last night.

"You *didn't* have regrets but you still took off?" he said as if that didn't make sense.

How much should she tell him? Should she tell him that by the time he'd fallen asleep this morning, in her mind they were a power couple—successful small-town business owners, married with two kids and a dog—and that she was mentally remodeling the little house to accommodate baby number three?

And that when she'd realized that's where her thoughts were going, she'd panicked?

That she'd panicked because she *hadn't* been able to convince herself that the idea was silly? Because it had struck her that that that was all something she suddenly might actually want with him?

That she'd panicked because as irrational as part of her brain had told her it was, she still hadn't been able to *believe* it was irrational and instead had seriously considered waking him up and telling him?

That she'd only hesitated when it had occurred

to her that he might think she'd lost her mind to be leaping ahead that far after one night together?

She'd wanted so much, and feared his rejection so deeply, that she hadn't been able to stay with him.

That seemed like too much to say.

So she said, "I was thinking about the future. As if us having a whole future together was just the next step—after one night—and I was afraid I was getting carried away."

Micah nodded slowly, calmly. "And that freaked you out."

"Because, for all I knew, last night was a one-night stand—"

"Not if it's up to me it wasn't."

That was music to her ears but Lexie went on without saying that. "I was fast-forwarding too far and I needed the voice of reason from Jill to push Stop."

Another simple nod of acceptance. "And Jill said what?"

"A lot."

"A lot that was good or bad?" he asked.

It was beginning to sink in that he wasn't upset with her, that he just didn't understand what had happened. But he was trying to, even though it seemed as if she might have hurt him a little by running away. That made her more inclined to try to explain herself.

"Jill said a lot that was good *and* bad. A while ago, Gram made a comment about what was old being new again with us. Jill kind of said the same thing. She said that there was still the old relationship as a sort of foundation between us, so already thinking about the future after one night together didn't sound strange to her. And she said a lot of things about feelings, destiny…"

Jill had said that maybe reconnecting and finding their way back to being friends and then moving from that into what had developed now, into the feelings Lexie had for Micah, into feelings Jill was convinced Micah had for Lexie, was a sign that they were meant to be together. That Jason and the rift over the barn incident was just destiny's way of sending them each in different directions to learn what they'd needed to learn, to grow in ways they'd needed to grow so that they could come together at last as the people they were meant to be. She'd said that regardless of how they'd gotten here, regardless of how long it had taken, regardless of how bumpy the road had been, when it was right, it was right.

It had been what Lexie had wanted to hear, what she hoped was true.

"And the bad?" Micah prompted.

"She asked me if I really could put everything behind me. If I could trust you—" *and happily spend my life with you* "—or would it all come back when the bloom was off this new rose. She wondered if we might have a fight and there it would all be again…"

"Would it?" he asked in a quiet voice.

"I hated you so much, for so long…"

"I know. I deserved it."

"And I still hate that you did what you did. But now that I understand it…and now that so much time has passed…it's like a balloon that's lost all its air. And you're so different… You've changed so much…" In all the ways she'd taken note of since coming home. "Getting to know the man you are now just makes it more clear that you were a big dumb, misguided kid then. And since I don't see any of that kid in you now, I'm sure that when you make me mad, I'll be mad at you, not at that boy—unless you revert to being that boy…"

"I can guarantee the Marines left him in the dust."

She thought so, too, because from what she'd seen—from what she could see standing there in front of her at that moment—the cockiness was gone and in its place was a genuine strength, someone confident enough in himself not to have to prove anything.

He was a man whose hotheadedness had been replaced by tolerance.

A man who had gone from self-centered to caring and insightful and thoughtful enough to have had that picture frame fixed for her.

He was a man who had put aside himself and everything he was working so hard for to help with the house repairs because he'd given his word that he would.

A man who had listened to her and put his mind to the task of helping her find her way.

"I can believe that the boy you were is long gone," she said. "I expected the worst from you and waited and watched for it to show itself, but it just isn't there anymore."

And little by little, the man he'd become had won her over.

"What about the trust part of it?" he asked.

"I wouldn't have thought it was possible but somehow that's come along with it all," she said, having realized the previous evening that trusting him was what had allowed her to let down her guard enough to spend the night with him. That she never could have if she *didn't* trust him.

"Did Jill have more to say on the bad side?" he asked.

"She said, *what about kids*," Lexie informed him. "She wondered if I had kids with you, would I look at you being a father to them and remember that what you did changed my relationship with my own dad."

Micah's handsome face sobered even more. "God, I never thought of that…"

"The voice of reason—that's why I needed to talk to Jill," Lexie said.

"Would it be bad?" he asked with dread in his tone, in his expression.

Lexie hadn't thought about the possibility, either. She'd only been thinking about how much it had impacted Micah to *not* have his baby born, and how touched she'd been by the story of it, how much she'd liked the idea of being the person to give him that family he knew he wanted now.

But when their friend had brought it up, she'd had to give it serious thought.

"What you did set the wheels into motion for what played out our senior year," Lexie said. "But when I really looked at it… All these years, it's been so much more neat and tidy to just wrap the rift with my dad into the package of blame I laid at your feet because what you did led to him finding out about Jason and me."

Micah nodded, accepting that blame yet again.

"But that's as far as your responsibility goes," she said then. "What really broke my dad and me apart was what I was doing…what Jason and I were doing. It was my own actions that disappointed my father, that made him look at me differently. I think I've taken the easy way out all this time by framing it as your fault. In all honesty, he probably would have found out sooner or later without you having anything to do with it. And he'd have felt the same way. Reacted the same way."

"So I get a little bit of absolution there?"

"You do. And I'm taking responsibility for what really set my dad off."

"And say you and I have kids…" Micah ventured cautiously.

The image of that, of Micah with a daughter she'd given him, brought some moisture to her eyes. "I'd try to make sure that you accepted it when your little girl grew up and wasn't just a little girl anymore," she said, sad that her father hadn't ever gotten to that point.

"Ah, Lexie…" Micah said, seeing the tears in her eyes. He pushed off the post with his shoulder and stepped closer, taking her into his arms to comfort her.

Again, he put her comfort first when he could have maintained his distance, could have agreed it was about time she let him off at least one hook and took some accountability herself, he could have been miffed at her for sneaking out on him.

No wonder she loved him. Now, today and from here on despite their history, despite the fact that this new chapter of their relationship had only just begun and she was relatively fresh from her marriage.

And even if it wasn't the same for him…

Because ultimately that had been what had really

sent her panic over the edge this morning—when she'd accepted that just because she'd developed feelings for him, it didn't mean he'd developed those same kind of feelings for her...

After a moment, Micah's arms around her loosened and he leaned back enough to look down at her again.

"Did Jill have any more bad things to say?"

"No." But even though their friend had bet her that Micah had fallen back in love with her, Lexie had been afraid to count on it.

Then he said, "It really shook me up when I found you gone this morning. But now that I know that it isn't because you went back to hating me—"

"No, not that..." she said wryly.

"It opened my eyes to some things, too... What if I said that as far as I'm concerned, you can go ahead and fast-forward for us all you want?"

Lexie merely raised her eyebrows at him, thinking it was time he did some of the talking, wanting to hear what he had to say before she revealed any more.

He went on to tell her about seeing Gertie this morning, about the fright he'd felt over finding Lexie gone. He told her it had led him to realize how he felt about her and all he wanted, too. It all sounded so much like what had sent Lexie into her tizzy that it almost made her smile.

"The crush I had on you passed and I've never

had another one—it really was a teenage thing. But I've also never felt before what I feel for you now—not about anyone," he said. "And something inside me just *knows* I'm only completely what I'm supposed to be when I'm with you..."

He sighed, dropped his head to the top of hers and seemed to gather strength before he said in a deep voice for her alone, "I'm in love with you, Lexie. I want to be your husband. I want to have kids with you. I want the rest of my life with you. But I want you any way you'll have me... If you need more time, I'll give you that. If you need space, I'll give you that." He paused and when he finished, his voice was even quieter, heavier. "But if you just don't feel the same way and you want me to step back and never bother you again...it'll kill me but that's what I'll do..."

Because he didn't know how she felt about him because she hadn't had the courage to be the first of them to say it.

"All the years with Jason, the divorce, feel surprisingly far away for me," she told him. "So I *sooo* don't want time or space," she said with a hint of a laugh, because even just the fact that his arms were loose around her put more distance between them than she wanted right now. "And I definitely don't want you to step back because I think that might kill me, too..."

He raised his head from hers and grinned down at her.

"Oh, thank God…" he muttered. And as if he'd been set free to say it with even more conviction, he said, "I love you, Lexie. Will you marry me?"

Relief washed over her. "I love you, too, Micah. And I will marry you."

His grin grew wide enough to put creases at the corners of those stellar blue eyes. "And promise me you will *never* make me wake up and wonder where you are again."

"Scared you, huh?"

"Terrified me. I was worried you really might be just using me."

"Well…" she teased as if that were even a possibility. The truth was that making love with him had been so tremendous she couldn't imagine never doing it again.

"Okay," he played along. "Use me all you want."

"Oh, I intend to," she assured him. His grin went even wider just before he gave her a kiss that seemed to claim her finally, once and for all, as his own.

It ended far too soon.

"But right now you need to call Gertie and let her know you're home and everything with us has smoothed out," he said.

"Tell me the truth—you just want me in order to get to my grandmother," Lexie joked again.

"Well…" he answered in the same teasing tone she'd used before. Then he said, "I'm all for the package deal."

But he delayed that call just a little longer by kissing her again.

And as Lexie indulged in it, in no hurry to do anything else, she marveled at where she was and who she was with—and how much she honestly did love this man.

This man who had somehow gone from the boy who had done her wrong to the person she couldn't imagine herself ever living without.

* * * * *

Don't miss the next book in
The Camdens of Montana miniseries,
available May 2021 from
Harlequin Special Edition!

WE HOPE YOU ENJOYED
THIS BOOK FROM

HARLEQUIN
SPECIAL
EDITION

Believe in love. Overcome obstacles. Find happiness.

Relate to finding comfort and strength in the
support of loved ones and enjoy the journey
no matter what life throws your way.

6 NEW BOOKS AVAILABLE EVERY MONTH!

COMING NEXT MONTH FROM

ⒽHARLEQUIN
SPECIAL EDITION

"And your secluded mountainside home with the
fancy electronics is part of that safety net? And your
hellhound?"

Jillie chuckled, looking up to where Sophie was
glaring down at Matt from the deck. "Don't insult my
dog. She's more for companionship than protection.
Although her appearance doesn't hurt." She shuddered
and pulled her jacket tighter.

God, he'd kept her standing out here in the cold and
dark while he grilled her with questions. She'd already
hinted that it was time for him to go. He scrubbed his
hands down his face.

"I'm sorry, Jillie. You must be freezing. Go on up.
Once I know you're inside, I'll take off."

"And you were on your way to dinner. You must
be starving." She hesitated for just a moment. In that
moment, he *really* wanted her to invite him up to join

her for dinner, but that didn't happen. Instead, she flashed him a quick smile before turning to go. "Thanks again, Matt."

Let her walk away. Way too complicated. Just let her walk away.

She was all the way up to the deck when he heard his own voice calling out to her.

"The old ski lift is working well, but I need to give it a few test runs, just to get acquainted with the thing. If you want a ride up to that craggy summit you like so much, I'll be heading up there Sunday afternoon. It'll just be us. No workers. No spectators."

Her head started to move back and forth, then stopped. She looked down at him in silence, then gave a loud sigh. "Maybe. I'll let you know. I've…I've got to go in."

He watched her and Sophie go through the door. She turned and locked it, then gave him a stuttering wave. For someone obsessed with privacy, it was interesting that this entire wall, right up to the peak of the A-frame roof, was glass. He lifted his hand, then headed to his car. He wasn't sure what surprised him more. That he'd asked Jillie to ride to the top of the mountain with him, or that she'd said maybe. As he turned the ignition, he realized he was smiling.

Get 4 FREE REWARDS!

We'll send you 2 FREE Books plus 2 FREE Mystery Gifts.

Harlequin Special Edition books relate to finding comfort and strength in the support of loved ones and enjoying the journey no matter what life throws your way.

FREE Value Over $20

YES! Please send me 2 FREE Harlequin Special Edition novels and my 2 FREE gifts (gifts are worth about $10 retail). After receiving them, if I don't wish to receive any more books, I can return the shipping statement marked "cancel." If I don't cancel, I will receive 6 brand-new novels every month and be billed just $4.99 per book in the U.S. or $5.74 per book in Canada. That's a savings of at least 12% off the cover price! It's quite a bargain! Shipping and handling is just 50¢ per book in the U.S. and $1.25 per book in Canada.* I understand that accepting the 2 free books and gifts places me under no obligation to buy anything. I can always return a shipment and cancel at any time. The free books and gifts are mine to keep no matter what I decide.

235/335 HDN GNMP

Name (please print)

Address   Apt. #

City   State/Province   Zip/Postal Code

Email: Please check this box ☐ if you would like to receive newsletters and promotional emails from Harlequin Enterprises ULC and its affiliates. You can unsubscribe anytime.

Mail to the **Reader Service:**
IN U.S.A.: P.O. Box 1341, Buffalo, NY 14240-8531
IN CANADA: P.O. Box 603, Fort Erie, Ontario L2A 5X3

Want to try 2 free books from another series? Call 1-800-873-8635 or visit www.ReaderService.com.

Love Harlequin romance?

DISCOVER.

Be the first to find out about promotions, news and exclusive content!

f Facebook.com/HarlequinBooks

🐦 Twitter.com/HarlequinBooks

📷 Instagram.com/HarlequinBooks

📌 Pinterest.com/HarlequinBooks

ReaderService.com

EXPLORE.

Sign up for the Harlequin e-newsletter and download a free book from any series at
TryHarlequin.com

CONNECT.

Join our Harlequin community to share your thoughts and connect with other romance readers!
Facebook.com/groups/HarlequinConnection

HSOCIAL2020

HARLEQUIN

Heartfelt or suspenseful, inspiring or passionate, Harlequin has your happily-ever-after.

With new books published every month, you are sure to find the satisfying escape you know you deserve.